RANCHER IN DANGER

BARB HAN

To my family for unwavering love and support. I can't imagine doing life with anyone else. I love you guys with all my heart.

1

itter, angry clouds rolled across an expansive Texas sky, threatening to unleash a catastrophic torrent and an end to a devastating two-year drought. Under normal circumstances, rain would be welcomed. But this storm wasn't the way to go about replenishing the earth. Besides, all Birdie West could focus on was the fact she would soon lose the grandmother she loved.

Tears threatened to fall at the thought of losing her only family. She blinked away the water welling in her eyes, causing the road to blur. She'd only passed two vehicles on the two-lane highway in the past forty-five minutes. Her trip to Lone Star Pass, Texas, wasn't a vacation or an escape. This trip was a favor to the woman who'd helped raise her. How the news she was about to bring to light would be received was anybody's guess. Who knew what kind of reception she would receive when she showed up at the Firebrand Ranch with a will in hand that left her grandmother—Meg as she preferred to be called—with enough money to pay for the care she needed and be more than comfortable for her remaining days.

Producing the will had been a last resort for Meg. Did she fear putting Birdie in the middle of a fight? The resignation in Meg's eyes when she stumbled over to the bedroom safe, a safe that had been well hidden for countless years, and produced the legal document had been apparent. So had the pain.

The sticky part was that if rich had a category, the Firebrands would be well above it. They would also have fancy lawyers that might tie up the money in court for years like Anna Nicole Smith experienced with her eighty-nine-year-old husband. Meg had never mentioned Marshall Firebrand to Birdie, so she had no idea what their relationship had been. The two could have been friends, except that didn't explain the large sum of money involved. All Birdie knew for certain was the man had wanted to leave a million dollars to someone he must've viewed as close to him at one time.

Then again, it was possible he'd fallen in love with Meg's art. At one time, she'd been one of the most prominent artists in Texas. Meg often teased that if she'd known she would live this long, she would have saved for retirement. Meg had saved. Then, she'd been deceived and wiped out by a man she'd trusted.

The two of them had been getting by okay once Birdie moved in. She'd been working two jobs to make ends meet. But this last medical setback was too much.

A crack of thunder shook the earth. A fawn bolted across the street. Birdie gasped, slammed on the brake, and cranked the steering wheel to the right. The hatchback missed the fawn but landed bumper down in a ditch.

Heart thundering, Birdie jumped into 'go' mode. Throwing her shoulder into the door as she pulled the handle, she practically fell out of the vehicle. The step down wasn't a good sign for being able to back her car out easily. She walked around the powder blue vehicle that she'd nicknamed 'Blue Jay.'

The way her bumper was wedged into the ditch left all four tires dangling in the air. There was no way she was going to be able to back out of this mess. Not ready to give up just yet, she opened the trunk to see if there was anything she could use.

There was a crowbar—which she grabbed—and for whatever reason, there was a blanket. It was far too hot to need a wool cover this time of year in Texas. Then she remembered using it for a picnic at the lake New Year's Eve, and a date that had ended a three-year relationship. As the saying went, *out with the old*. At least, that had been Ethan's motto. After three years together, he finally confessed that for the past twelve months he'd been in love with someone from work. How great was it that he'd strung her along while he was courting another woman?

The thought still burned. Looking back, she should have seen the writing on the wall. All those times he'd had to stay late at work. Then, there were the last-minute canceled plans. His sudden reluctance to plan a vacation together should have been a big clue. But she'd trusted Ethan. She'd believed him when he'd told her that starting a new job as a financial advisor meant he needed to work long hours. She'd supported him, told him how proud she was of his commitment to a new career path.

And then he'd paid her back by sleeping with an intern while she'd been watching shows like *Say Yes To The Dress*. To be fair, she'd never been the type to dream of her wedding day. At least, not until she'd seen an engagement ring tucked inside a box in his backpack when he stayed over Thanksgiving. Christmas had come and gone, along with the day she thought he would propose. After, she'd decided the ring would be unboxed at New Year's.

Nope. Turned out, the ring wasn't meant for her. Ethan had planned to propose to his girlfriend Isabella, or Izzy to her friends. Okay, so Birdie had gone down a rabbit hole and stalked Izzy's social media after a second glass of wine on New Year's Day. Then, she'd told herself to move on.

When she got out of the ditch, she made a mental note to burn the blanket. In the meantime, she needed to see if there was anything else she could use inside the vehicle. As she walked around the back of Blue Jay, she saw a truck headed her way.

Birdie stepped up to the small shoulder of the paved road. She could only hope the driver of the truck wasn't a maniac or rapist, considering she was stranded on the side of the road.

The engine hummed, and she heard a door open and close.

"How'd you manage that?" A tall, muscled stranger lifted the ballcap he was wearing enough to air out his head as he stood on the side of the road next to his truck, emergency flashers blinking a staccato rhythm.

A wise guy?

"This? Figured I'd measure the ditch. See how deep it was, so I drove it right in," Birdie shot back, gripping her cell.

"Good thinking," he said, turning around like he was about to leave the scene without so much as offering a hand. Seriously?

It was fine, or *would* be fine. She didn't need his help anyway. She'd been in worse pickles than this and figured a way out. Still, it galled her to think he wouldn't at least offer.

"Nice. Go. I got this," she mumbled under her breath.

She threw her hands up in the air without tossing her cell phone away, and said, "Unbelievable," before returning a balled fist to her hip. Let the man go on his way.

This was the point where she needed to call in a tow truck, but it galled her to have to spend money she didn't have to spare. At least, not yet. Once she laid claim to the Firebrand inheritance on behalf of Grandma Meg, there would be plenty of money to go around. Of course, Birdie didn't care about taking someone else's money.

She kicked her back tire. The lack of rain made for dry dirt, but the way her car was wedged in the ditch would make it impossible shift into reverse and drive out. The skies threatened to open up any minute now. Wouldn't that be icing on the cake?

The truck didn't pull away, as expected. What was this guy doing? She reached inside her vehicle to locate her cell as the sound of his voice traveled over and through her, creating an unexpected warmth in her.

"Yes, it's me. Fallon." He paused a beat. "I know. It's been a long time. I'm coming home now, though." Another pause. "Yes, for good this time." More silence. "I'm not kidding. I'm done with the service."

He walked around the back of his truck and then leaned against the bumper. The fact he'd been in the military explained his tight clipped haircut and the way he stood with his back ramrod straight. Don't get her started on his muscles. Those proved he held himself to a higher standard than most when it came to working out. The five o'clock shadow on his chiseled granite face had thrown her off. But it was, in fact, close to dinner time.

∼

"Any chance you can swing by and help?" Fallon Firebrand asked Bronc Harris, who was on the phone. The ranch foreman had worked for the Marshall for years. The last time Fallon had seen Bronc, he'd been in his late fifties with weather-worn skin and a permanent tan.

"Give me the location and I'll head on over," Bronc said, a strain in his voice. He'd always been a worrier and it was reassuring that not everything had changed. Losing his employer must have been a huge hit.

"Hold on a sec." Fallon checked GPS on his phone, took a pic of their location and sent it over. He had to love technology. "Should be arriving in your text messages any sec—"

The delivered notification cut him off.

"Got it," Bronc said. "I'll head on over."

"I appreciate it," Fallon said, figuring there'd be time for explanations and reunion talk later.

"It's good to have you home," Bronc said.

"Good to be back," Fallon admitted before ending the call. Granted, he wasn't exactly home yet, but he'd made it to Lone Star Pass and that was pretty much the same thing. The minute he drove through town, he was hit with a bout of nostalgia.

Fallon grabbed a stack of cones from the back of his new truck. He'd ordered the pickup and a few supplies so he'd have a few basics. He had very little in the way of belongings. Pretty much everything he wanted to bring back fit inside his duffel. Once a rancher, always a rancher and that meant being prepared for almost anything. In his former line of work 'almost anything' had an annoying habit of showing up at the most inconvenient times. In the military, he was almost guaranteed it would.

He placed cones on the road, spacing them three feet apart. This way, anyone speeding down the road would have a heads-up to slow down. Folks sometimes confused themselves with Indy drivers on this stretch. He wanted them to be warned of possible dangers ahead in time to find their brakes.

When he was done, he joined the driver. Since he didn't see another vehicle around, he needed to see if she slurred her words or seemed to be on any type of medication that might have caused her to veer off the road.

The woman stood there with her arms folded across her chest, staring at her vehicle from various angles. Her stiff posture gave him the impression she needed a minute. She looked to be in her late twenties with auburn hair that had black tips that fell soft around her face and barely touched her shoulders. Her hair reminded him of everything he loved about fall color. Big brown eyes that made him think of autumn leaves were hooded by thick lashes. She had full, pink lips that begged to be kissed. Lips he had no business letting his gaze linger on.

"Birdie West," she said, spinning toward him and then sticking her hand out between them. She wore a tank top, jean shorts, and boots.

"Fallon." He took the hand being offered and shook, ignoring the trill of electricity that shot through him the minute they made physical contact. His reaction caught him off guard.

"Are you from around here?" he asked, already breaking a sweat and he hadn't done any heavy lifting yet. The humidity was off the charts despite the fact not a droplet of rain had fallen so far. The threat was certainly there. Mother Nature needed to get it together.

"You got a last name?" Birdie asked with a small head shake. Her pulse thumped at the base of her throat, and she seemed nervous. She brought her hand up to cover her neck, a sure sign she was feeling vulnerable. Then again, she was alone and stranded on a country road. Was she afraid of him?

To ease the tension, he took a few steps toward the vehicle and dropped down on one knee like he was examining the ditch situation. He remembered the threat to the ranch and decided against revealing his parentage for the time being. "Just Fallon. Is Birdie a nickname?"

"No. I'm just Birdie," she said.

"Well, Birdie, help is on the way," he stated, making himself as small as possible, which was difficult for a man of his size to do. "I called a friend."

"I heard," she said. "Thank you."

The fact she hadn't stopped him from making the call made him believe she wasn't from these parts. She would have already made the call herself if she was. She would have waved him on and told him someone was on the way to help. Her eyes were clear and her speech seemed fine. All good signs this was an honest mistake.

"Mind if I ask where you're from?" He was mostly making small talk, except a part of him wanted to know if he had a chance of ever seeing her again once she was out of the ditch for reasons he couldn't explain.

Maybe it had to do with the fact that she was new in town and after talking to Eric, Fallon realized how much everything had probably changed. It might be nice to have someone he could talk to who didn't have any involvement with his family.

"South of Austin," she said. "Small town."

"We had a friend who moved to Austin after she graduated high school. I heard she's doing great things in country music lately," he said for lack of anything better. He was normally a better talker than this but Birdie had his tongue-tied. This seemed like a good time to remind himself he was no longer an awkward teenager. He'd grown tall in middle school, but it had taken a while to fill out his frame. His brothers and cousins bulked up long before Fallon, but he'd grown into his frame during his military service.

"Isn't Raleigh Perry originally from these parts?" The disbelief in Birdie's voice made him smile. He also realized he'd just found common ground. Talking might help Birdie relax. It bothered him that she could possibly feel physically threatened by him.

"That's who I'm referring to," he said.

"*You* know *her*?" Birdie's face twisted up. "I don't believe you."

Her reaction made him chuckle. Plus, he'd known Raleigh forever and hadn't seen her in longer than that, so it was impossible to think of her as some superstar.

Birdie seemed offended. "What?"

"It's been a long time since I've been home or seen anyone from here but, yes, I've known Raleigh since we were both this high." He held his hand up to around the waistband of his jeans.

"Seriously?" she asked, far more impressed now. "She has this amazing song…" She snapped her fingers together and then started humming.

"Are you talking about *The Loft*?" he asked, recognizing the tune.

"Yes, that's the one. You know it?" she asked, and he could almost see the neurons firing in her brain.

"It's my personal favorite," he admitted. "That one made it all the way overseas with my unit, which is where I've been for more than a decade."

"Thank you for your service," Birdie said, those blue eyes studying him like she was trying to figure him out.

"You're welcome," he said. His response was almost autopilot, but he meant it every time.

"Then you must be from around here originally," she noted.

"This is my childhood home," he said before walking around the perimeter of the hatchback to start coming up with a plan to get this baby out of the ditch and back on the road once Bronc arrived. Of course, a piece of him didn't mind sticking around and talking to Birdie despite the near-oppressive heat. It had been worse where he'd been stationed overseas. He would think he would have gotten used to it by now.

"Are you visiting relatives then?" she asked.

"More like coming home for good." He stepped in the ditch so she would be looking down at him from where she stood. She'd gotten herself in an interesting position as she'd driven almost straight in, perpendicular to the road. Now, that she seemed to be more comfortable with him, he figured it was safe to ask about the accident without her shutting down. "Mind if I ask what happened here?"

"Did you hear that thunder boom earlier?" she asked.

He nodded. It had practically rocked the road. "The one that felt more like an earthquake?"

"Yes," she agreed. "A fawn shot of nowhere because of it. I slammed on the brakes and turned the steering wheel a little too hard. Went straight in and left myself no feasible way to get out without a tow truck."

"Looks like the fawn lived." He glanced around.

"Thankfully," she said, then motioned toward the hatchback. "Blue Jay didn't do so hot."

He shook his head and pursed his lips together to keep from commenting on the name she'd given her vehicle. It was kind of adorable, and he didn't want to like this stranger any more than he already did.

"Are you passing through town or planning to stick around?" he asked, searching for good attachment points on the vehicle for when Bronc showed. The trick to successfully recovering a stuck car was finding good attachment points.

"I have business here," she said. "Only planning on staying long enough to settle it, which hopefully won't take much time."

"What kind of business?" he asked.

"Personal. I'm on a mission for Meg..." She seemed to realize he would have no idea who that was. "My grandmother."

"She couldn't come with you?" he asked, and then regretted the question almost as soon as it came out of his mouth when he saw her body tense up like she'd just taken a punch. He'd clearly struck a nerve. "You don't have to answer that."

"She isn't well," Birdie said with a frown that nearly cut his heart out of his chest. She quickly recovered. Then, said, "You never said your last name."

No, he hadn't. And he had no plans to, so he needed to think his way out of this real quick. A crack of thunder caused them both to duck and think about running for cover. The sky rumbled, creating the distraction he needed. But was it enough to keep his identity a secret a little while longer?

2

"Do you want to sit inside my truck until Bronc gets here?"

Birdie nodded, figuring this guy couldn't possibly be a serial killer or he would have made his move by now. They were alone on a stretch of road that didn't seem like it had a whole lot of traffic. He'd already called for help and, besides, there was something honest about his eyes.

He opened the passenger door, so she thanked him and climbed inside. It was the neatest cab she'd ever sat in. There were no fast-food wrappers. The dashboard was impeccable. The floormats looked brand new.

Oh, right. Military.

When she really thought about it, the tidiness made sense. One of her friends from high school had served, and she'd noted how the kid who used to be a slob suddenly took care of everything, including himself, differently after his release.

Lightning lit the dark gray sky in an electric show that

looked a whole lot better from inside a vehicle where she couldn't get zapped. Still, no rain.

"Are you staying in town overnight?" Fallon asked, and then put a hand up like he realized how that might sound. "All I was going to suggest is that you stay at Conley Inn. It has a lot of fresh flowers and lace everywhere and Mrs. Conley cooks up some pretty mean waffles."

"I didn't see it when I checked online," she said, with an awkward shrug. "Sounds nice." And expensive. She hadn't bothered to do a thorough search. Her next-to-nothing budget would have her sleeping at a campground in her vehicle tonight. It was only for one night. She hoped.

He grabbed his cell phone and pulled up the map feature. His eyebrows drew together.

"Guess I haven't been home in a while. The Conley Inn closed three years ago," he said on a sharp sigh. "Shame."

"The waffles sounded pretty amazing. Too bad," she said. The place would most likely have been out of her price range anyway, despite Meg being the soon-to-be beneficiary of a million dollars. Plus, it wasn't like the money was in hand, or potentially ever would be. Meg had warned Birdie the family was powerful and might not be thrilled about Meg's relationship with Marshall. Birdie was willing to roll up her sleeves for a fight if it was fair. Sometimes, walking away was the only logical option.

Meanwhile, she considered herself more the living paycheck-to-paycheck type. Staring down her thirtieth birthday this year was a real wake-up call. It made her realize she wasn't where she thought she would be at this age. What was it about those birthdays ending in a zero that caused people to reevaluate their life choices?

Granted, she'd been helping Meg financially instead of building her own nest egg. Actually, she'd wiped out her savings and the hope of starting her own small business before age thirty while trying to keep up with the cost of Meg's prescriptions, co-pays, and random medical bills. But Birdie would do it all again if it made her grandmother more comfortable or bought more time, no questions asked.

"Yeah, I guess a whole lot has changed around here," he said and there was a melancholy note to his voice.

"Seems like a nice enough place," she offered. "And I know a thing or two about change."

"Life is full of unscheduled right turns," he stated, and then seemed to realize the reference fit a little too well in her circumstance.

"Tell me about it," she said with a smile. Then, she laughed. She couldn't help it. All the tension that had been coiled inside of her for days—weeks?—released with an exhale as she laughed harder. "Sorry. Nothing about this situation is funny. It's just sometimes the only thing left to do is laugh."

He chuckled and it was a low rumble from deep in his chest. He had the kind of deep timbre that traveled over her and through her, surprising her. There was something about this man that made her feel chaotic and calm at the same time. Like a storm was brewing inside her but she was somehow in the eye. He stirred up feelings she'd shelved after Ethan, figuring she wouldn't be going down that road anytime soon. Ever? And yet, this felt different. Different from her ex. Different from anyone in her past. Different from anything she'd ever known. She balanced in that place between embracing the chaos and fearing it.

"It's been a long time since I've seen someone wedge themselves into a ditch quite so artfully," he teased like he was trying to keep the mood light.

"Really? I would think that happened all the time out

here in the sticks," she shot back, needing a good release. Humor was the best medicine.

The two laughed until her sides hurt.

"None of this is funny. You do realize that, right?" she asked, trying to rein it in without much luck.

"I do," he said.

She laughed so hard, she snorted. Realizing what just happened caused her to double snort. "I need to stop. It's really not funny."

When he turned to look at her, laughing suddenly became the last thing on her mind; her throat dried up and her tongue felt like she'd just licked a glue stick. She coughed, trying to cover and somehow ease the dryness, but it didn't work. The air in the vehicle charged with electricity.

A truck came into view, which was just the distraction she needed. It was coming directly at them, headlights flashing. This must be the help Fallon had called for.

"You're welcome to stay inside the cab, or help. Either way, it's your choice," he said, and she appreciated that he didn't treat her like a fragile doll.

"My car. My fault it's in the ditch," she said by way of explanation as she exited his truck. The air was thick outside, but nothing in comparison to what had just happened inside the cab of his vehicle. Birdie tried to shake it off, reminding herself that she had a job to do. She would get in and get out of town as soon as she met with the family and delivered a copy of the will.

There was probably no way a rich family was going to be happy about losing a million dollars to a stranger. Meg had said this was her ticket out, and the only way she could repay Birdie for all the money she was spending plus some. Meg had said the nest egg would ease her last few months on this earth and allow her to give Birdie enough seed money to stick with her plan of starting her own business. It was supposed to be a win-win. Honestly, all Birdie wanted was for Meg to be happy and out of pain. There didn't need to be money left over. The business could wait. She was young and, despite her birthday trying to tell her differently, she had her whole life in front of her.

Birdie didn't know a lot of wealthy families where she lived. But it didn't take a rocket scientist to realize the Firebrands wouldn't want to part with any of their inheritance. All the recent press about them seemed good, but they could be monsters behind closed doors. Who knew what they were really like?

FALLON GREETED Bronc with a bear hug.

"It sure is good to have you home," Bronc said after quickly introducing himself to Birdie.

"Good to be back," Fallon said, and meant it. No matter what changes were bound to come his way, he would be ready. It was time to dig his heels in and accept his place on the ranch built by his family and that had been generations in the making. "Have you been up to see Dad?"

"Yes, sir," Bronc said. The show of respect seemed to catch Birdie off guard. It was his fault. Fallon hadn't wanted to give away the fact he was a Firebrand. He'd wanted to hold onto that little piece of him that was Fallon and not his last name. Folks treated him differently when he was in Texas, especially Lone Star Pass residents. Overseas, he'd been given the nickname Tex—not exactly original—it had meant being treated like every other enlisted man. Despite the heat and the hardships, blending in and being treated like a normal person had been the best time of Fallon's life. It had been the reason four years had turned into twelve. He'd enlisted days after his twentieth birthday.

Birdie seemed to fixate on a bumper sticker on Bronc's vehicle. She turned to Fallon. "How do you know this family?"

"You could say they're very close to my heart," he stated.

"How close?" she continued.

"Should we pull your car from the ditch or stand around chatting?" he asked, trying to be nonchalant even though he heard the strain in his own voice.

"By all means," she said, motioning toward her hatchback but the lightness from a few minutes ago disintegrated before his eyes and a wall had come up in its place.

Was it so wrong of him to want to be a normal person in her eyes for just a little while longer? He seriously doubted she would know his last name if she was someone who was barely stopping in town. Then again, his family was big business in the town. Was it possible she was visiting the ranch?

Bronc went straight to work, and Fallon aided. He helped Bronc secure the straps, and then discuss the positioning of the truck that would pull the hatchback out.

"That should do it," Bronc said when they'd secured her straps. "I'll just pull around and we can attach the other side to my truck."

"Sounds like a plan," Fallon said.

The sky might be lighting up but Birdie had gone all kinds of quiet on him. To be fair, he should have told her who he was from the get-go. But, living in this fantasy a little bit longer had been too attractive to give up. Fallon wanted to be normal for just a little while on his return to a place that knew everything about him from the time he was born.

"Almost there," he said to Birdie, who'd been standing a couple of feet behind them while staring at her phone.

She barely glanced up when she said, "Good. Thanks."

They'd replaced real conversation with two-word answers. Her tone of voice said she was done talking.

"No problem," was all he could think to say, scratching his head as to the change in her tone.

Bronc repositioned his truck and they attached the straps to his end. It didn't take long for Blue Jay to be freed and back on the road.

"Will I see you back at the barn?" Bronc asked. He never did like going into the main house no matter how many times he'd been told that he was welcome.

"Tomorrow morning," Fallon said. "Unless you're willing to show at dinner."

"See you tomorrow," Bronc said with a smile. "He'll be all right. Your father is a strong person. He won't let this setback put him on the bench for long."

Bronc had definitely aged ten years. Or maybe it was just the worry lines creasing his forehead that threw Fallon off.

"He's strong," Fallon agreed. He wasn't exactly sure how he felt about his father after all the news he'd learned before making the drive here from San Antonio. Then there was the fact that Fallon didn't feel like he knew much about the man before signing up to serve to begin with. In this case, absence hadn't made the heart grow fonder. Fallon's mother was another story. His love for her ran deep. But then, she'd been the kind of mother most people only dreamed of having. She'd loved her boys more than anything despite making it known more than once that she wouldn't have minded throwing a daughter in the mix.

Birdie thanked both of them before claiming the driver's seat of her hatchback. The trucks were in her way and needed to be cleared out for her to continue down the road. When he really thought about it, the road led to his family's ranch. There wasn't much more out this way save for an RV park and campsite.

"I'll catch up with you later," Fallon said to Bronc. He didn't want Birdie to get away without saying a proper good-bye. She stirred something inside him that was probably best left dormant. Call him a sucker, but he wanted to figure out what it was before she disappeared from his life forever.

"See you back at the ranch," Bronc said. He saluted toward Birdie before disappearing into the cab of his truck and banking a U-turn.

Fallon walked over to the driver's side of Blue Jay. "Any chance you have dinner plans?"

"You never did answer my question," she said, studying him carefully.

He played dumb despite the fact he could almost promise he knew what she was about to ask.

"What's your last name?" she asked.

"Firebrand," he confirmed. At this point, they both knew.

"Why didn't you tell me that before?" she asked, a look of betrayal overtook her features.

"Because there's a whole lot that comes with the name, and I wanted to be just Fallon a little bit longer." He had no idea why he'd just blabbered on about his personal problem except to say that he wanted to explain himself to Birdie. He cared about whether or not she understood his reasoning.

"Interesting," she said in a tone that was unreadable.

"Is that a problem?" he continued.

Lightning subsided and it didn't look like they weren't going to get the storm Mother Nature seemed to be threatening.

"Why would I care who you are?" She shrugged her shoulder like the admission didn't bother her one bit, but her eyes gave her away this time.

And then it dawned on him why she might be affected.

"Who do you have business with while you're in town?" he asked.

"I guess you'll find out soon enough. Thanks for the help, though. I mean it. I would still be stuck here if it wasn't for you." She put the gearshift in reverse and then backed away from him before he could come up with a good reason for her to stick around. A second later, she zipped around his truck in the direction of the ranch.

Meeting Birdie had been an unexpected detour in his travels today. After hearing all the goings on at the ranch, some good, some not so much, he'd never felt so disconnected to his family as he did on the way home. It was evident that a whole lot had changed since he left. Change was inevitable. So, why was it bothering him so much that everything would be different?

Home, he thought. It was the one place that he'd hoped would be the same as when he left. There was something about the idea of home that had kept him going when his body wanted to quit and all he had left was sheer willpower to get through a day, a mission. He'd matured since he left town years ago, barely twenty and still wet behind the ears.

When work got to him, though, it was his mother's famous meatballs that he thought about tasting again. Those meatballs had gotten him out of more than one sticky situation and kept him focused on what he loved about his old life, what he would be returning to someday. There were times when he'd decided to make it back to the base, and eventually home, because he had to taste those meatballs again. He would envision them on one of his mother's white porcelain plates. She said food looked better when 'presented' on a blank canvas. He would think about the way the smell filled the house while the sauce slow-cooked, and how starved he would be after being inside for a few hours waiting for dinner.

Strange how those little details in life were the exact things he missed the most.

And, yes, he thought about hanging out with his brothers, a few of his cousins, and all the good times they had growing up. His father and the Marshall weren't exactly Fallon's favorite people. He didn't know them well enough to truly hate them. Mostly, he felt indifferent.

His thoughts circled back to the mysterious woman with auburn hair.

Fallon figured someone at home would know what Birdie wanted. It wouldn't be difficult to ask around. He put away the last of the orange hazard cones, and then reclaimed the driver's seat.

Home was an interesting concept to him now that he'd been away for so long. Was the saying true? Or could he go back?

3

Birdie could only hope the rest of the Firebrands were as decent and kind as Fallon. Forget the fact that the man was so smokin' hot she practically had to fan herself when he was within arm's reach. Her entire body had warmed anytime he got close. Too bad she wasn't the one-night-stand type because he was exactly the kind of person she would...

She stopped herself right there, erasing all sinning on Sunday thoughts. He might very well end up being the enemy. If Meg's will was contested and ended up in court, she would have to sit on the other side of a courtroom with him. There was no way she could see herself opposing this man in a court of law after seeing him naked and vice versa. But then, why was she even thinking casual sex was an option with Fallon Firebrand?

Stress, came the answer. She'd been under pressure, which was fine. It wasn't anything she couldn't handle. Well, everything except the part where she was going to lose Meg. Tears welled just thinking about the reality.

No, Meg needed to live many more years. And as long as

Birdie was making wishes, she wanted Meg to be pain free. Life was strange when Birdie really thought about it. Everything had been going well and ticking along just like normal. She'd been working two jobs saving up enough money to rent a small space in Austin so she could launch her gourmet doughnut shop.

Life had other plans.

Meg was diagnosed with liver cancer and life became about choices. Birdie didn't regret hers. She would throw every dime she had into a fund if it made Meg's life easier or longer. There was no question about it.

When Birdie's mother had suddenly died, Meg had been there. She'd taken Birdie in for her last couple years of high school, given her a place to call home when her world had been turned upside-down. Meg had been a rock. Seeing her fragile and in pain hurt Birdie's soul.

Getting the Firebrand family to honor Marshall's wishes meant so much more than financial security. It meant Birdie could repay a little bit of the kindness Meg had shown. It meant Birdie could show Meg how important she was. And it meant Birdie could focus on living out her last few months without worrying about how to pay the bills.

The money Meg had promised to Birdie had no bearing. Birdie intended to return every dime that wasn't used on medical services or care. Birdie could rebuild her savings. She'd done it once. She could do it again. The gourmet doughnut shop idea would still be there in a couple of years when Birdie had the cash. If it wasn't for her thirtieth birthday staring her in the face, she wouldn't feel any pressure at all.

She would figure it out and make do just like she always did. Like when Micky Castle had asked her to prom and she refused to let Meg buy a dress. Birdie had gone on YouTube and figured out how to embellish a simple dress in her closet. Micky's reaction when she'd opened the door to greet him had been priceless. The dress had turned out beautifully and she'd felt good in it. Not only was it gorgeous, but she hadn't spent a fortune on it. Win-win.

Losing her mother at the age of fifteen had knocked the wind out of her. Meg had been her safe landing. It was time to pay Meg back.

Birdie pulled into the RV park. This place wasn't too far from the Firebrand Ranch, and had a camping area complete with shower and bathroom facilities. Twelve dollars a night was a whole lot cheaper than anything else in the area and she didn't mind sleeping in her car very much. The seat reclined. She had blankets and a pillow, not that she needed a heavy blanket in August when the temps were in the low eighties overnight. The trick was waking up with the sun, immediately showering to cool off, and getting to a diner or coffee shop before the real heat hit. Triple digit temperatures were nothing to take lightly despite being a lifelong Texan.

Staying inside in A/C during the heat of the day made the nights bearable.

Her thoughts circled back to Fallon, and the disappointed look on his face when she realized he was a Firebrand. It wasn't her fault that he hadn't volunteered the information sooner that was a complete game-changer. She forced him from her mind as she texted Meg to let her know she'd made it to her destination.

Meg visiting a small town like this one was almost unthinkable. And yet, she'd traveled all over the state. She'd been commissioned to create southwestern art pieces for the airport, large banks, and dozens of private citizens whose names remained in locked files—files Meg said needed to be burned after her death and never unsealed. First of all, Birdie couldn't even imagine a world without Meg in it. Secondly, whose names were in those files? Birdie's imagination ran wild, and she wondered how many secrets were inside.

The will hadn't come from inside a locked filing cabinet. This secret had been inside a hidden safe.

Of course, Meg would have such a thing. When Birdie really thought about it, she expected no less from a woman who'd charted her own territory as an installation artist and free spirit. The free spirit part had been very savvy, though. Until Christopher had come along and taken advantage of Meg.

Birdie fumed just thinking about the betrayal. Meg had been in love. On her side, the relationship had been everything she'd ever dreamed of. It had been real. The way Meg had gushed over Christopher should have been Birdie's first clue the man was up to no good. No one was that perfect. He'd said all the right things. Done all the right things. He'd made Meg feel like the only person in the world, or so she'd said. He'd been a hopeless romantic and for a little while Meg was the happiest Birdie had ever seen her. All the while he was bilking her out of her life savings.

Birdie smacked her flat palm against the steering wheel. She would never fall for the perfect man because there was no such thing. Real people had flaws. Of course, Ethan hadn't been much better than Christopher. Her ex had broken her heart. Although, looking back, perhaps he'd hurt her pride more than anything else.

Now that she'd checked out her nighttime accommodations, she was ready to tackle her next objective...the Firebrand family. It was getting late. The skies had cleared up but the air was still thick. The words *humidity* and *Texas* didn't use to belong in the same sentence. There should be a ground soaking with this level of humidity instead of all this threat and nothing to back it up. The worst part was the lack of rain. They needed a good downpour.

Hunger pangs reminded her it had been a long time since lunch, so she decided the Firebrands could wait a few more minutes. She parked near the facilities, and then grabbed her lunchbox. The sandwich held up nicely and reminded her of middle school when she'd insisted on peanut butter and jelly sandwiches every day for lunch. The cool apple felt good on her parched throat. She opened a bottled water and drained the contents. There were graham crackers. Wow, this really was a middle school lunch. But, hey, she'd never been afraid to have a bowl of Cheerios for dinner after a long day, so this was practically gourmet. Besides, she was hungry and this meal did the trick. All she needed now was a cookie to complete the lunchbox food.

Actually, a chocolate chip cookie sounded amazing about now. Birdie sighed when she glanced over at the kitchen supply catalog she'd forgotten was inside her vehicle. She'd forgone buying a new car in order to save for an industrial-sized oven for her shop. No regrets. Her new motto served her well and she needed to remember it often. Her priorities had shifted now and for a good cause.

Once she got Meg situated, and Birdie could only think of a scenario where Meg's health improved, she could resume plans for a future—a future that involved Meg being alive and well.

And everyone believed in miracles, right?

With a sigh, Birdie tucked the magazine underneath the seat on the passenger side. It was probably best not to spend too much time looking at it for now. Later, she could pick up where she left off.

After finishing her meal, she should probably swing by the Firebrands'. Birdie checked the map again, and then set her GPS. She kicked up a little bit of dust on the way out before turning onto the road to the ranch.

Her palms suddenly felt warm and sweaty at the notion of seeing Fallon again. It was unlikely. He was only just getting home and situated. He had a large family from what she'd read. Don't even get her started on how many cousins were in the brood and living on ranch property. What had she read? Something like eighteen in total. But there was something special about Fallon that she'd noticed right away. Seriously? Birdie couldn't afford to get distracted, no matter how handsome, kind, and perfect the man had seemed.

FALLON FIGURED he could sleep at his place tomorrow. Tonight, he wanted to stay in the main house and get caught up on everything that had been going down lately.

He had questions.

So many questions.

There were more questions swirling around in his mind than bees on a hive.

And yet, despite everything he'd heard so far, his thoughts still kept cycling back to a certain stranded motorist. Birdie West.

He could bring in his duffel bag later, he thought as he parked near the front of the house his grandfather had lived in. He exited the vehicle and walked to the porch, standing there for a moment soaking in the fact everything would be different now. It was still a shock to think anyone but the Marshall lived here. His grandfather had been set in his ways and stubborn as a mule, and one hundred percent associated with this home that was way too big for one person to live in. Despite their differences and lack of relationship, Fallon couldn't help but take a hit in the chest at the thought his grandfather was gone.

Adam and his wife and child living here was good. The place needed new life, he thought as he reached for and then turned the doorknob. Fallon immediately noticed the difference in atmosphere as he walked in the front door and noticed on his right that the old stuffy dining room had been turned into a bright and colorful playroom. The change was much-needed and a whole lot shocking to his system. 'Bout time, though.

There was no reason this place shouldn't have held lively Thanksgiving meals and Christmas mornings filled with laughter and rowdiness. Granted, him and his siblings could be a handful. But what was the point of having such a big house if not to fill it with the pitter-patter of little feet?

Fallon was waxing nostalgic but he did feel a sense of melancholy at all the lost opportunities in his grandfather's life. Then again, the Marshall had been set in his ways. He'd done things his way even though his face held a permanent scowl. Fallon couldn't help but wonder if the man's life would have been so much better if he'd opened his heart and his home to his grandchildren. The sad reality it was too late to find out now struck like another physical blow.

The sounds of laughter coming from the kitchen were a welcome distraction from Fallon's heavy thoughts. He made his way down the hallway and into the kitchen in time to walk in on his brother Adam taking his bride for a trip around the 'dance' floor. For a split second he didn't want to intrude on the happy couple. The gurgle sound of a baby in the background was about the cutest thing. But it was too late because his newly minted sister-in-law saw him and stopped.

"You must be Fallon," she said. "I'm Prudence."

He met her halfway across the room and stuck out his hand. She smiled at the gesture and hugged him anyway.

"Right. We're family now," he said with a smile, realizing just how silly he'd been trying to shake her hand.

"I never used to be a hugger until I joined this family," she admitted, her cheeks flush. She had a warmth and brightness to her smile. "Now, I'm hooked."

She sidestepped, allowing her husband to take over. Adam brought Fallon into a bear of a hug.

"It's good to see you again, man," Adam said. He pulled back and tucked his chin to his chest. Was Adam getting emotional?

"You, too. And congratulations," Fallon said. Being back in the Marshall's home might have struck him square in the chest, but there was a warmth that accompanied the happy family he saw here. "I like what you've done with the place."

"Thank you, and you're welcome to stay here if your house isn't ready," Adam said. "This is a shared space. We lay no claim to it."

"It suits you both." Fallon looked around. "All three of you, I should say."

"Do you want to meet your niece?" Adam practically beamed with pride when he glanced over at the little girl.

"Is that a real question?" Fallon walked over to the chair where the baby was strapped into a carrier-looking thing. He had no idea what kind of paraphernalia came with babies. She was all big cheeks and slobber, but he had to admit she was a cutie.

"She has your hair," Fallon teased. His joke netted an elbow jab in the ribcage.

"Oh yeah? She smells just like you a couple times a day," Adam shot back.

"Remind me not to ask when," Fallon said, wrinkling his nose. "Because she just smiled, grunted, and now we need to open a window."

Adam laughed as Prudence came over and joined them.

"I'll take her to clean her up and then spend some quality time in the playroom," she said. "Make yourself at home."

"It was good to meet you, Prudence," he said.

"You, too." She unbuckled the baby before gently lifting her out of the carrier. "I hope you stay."

The comment caught him off guard.

"That's the idea," he said. "But, first, coffee."

Prudence nodded toward a machine on the counter before excusing herself.

"She seems like a good person," Fallon said to his brother as he made his way across the kitchen. "Looks like you found someone to keep you in line."

"You have no idea, bro," Adam joked as he went to work beside Fallon, pulling a pair of mugs from the cabinet while Fallon got busy with the coffee machine, filling the carafe with water. "Fair warning, everyone says there's something in the water here. Everyone who drinks it seems to end up engaged or married."

Fallon made a show of pouring the water down the drain.

"Nice, but you do need water to make coffee," Adam seemed to feel the need to point out.

"Then, coffee water doesn't count." Fallon filled the carafe again and went back to work.

"You know how to work the machine there, buddy?" Adam teased as Fallon stood in front of it, staring.

"I've never met a coffee maker that I couldn't outsmart," he quipped. True to his word, he produced two cups in a matter of minutes.

Adam took a sip, and said, "Not bad, little bro."

"I picked up a few skills in the last decade," he responded, lifting his mug in salute.

"And change," Adam corrected.

"It really has been that long, hasn't it?" Fallon didn't bother to hide his embarrassment.

"Afraid so." Adam nodded and compressed his lips. The corners of his mouth turned down in a frown. He quickly recovered. "But you're here now. Did you mean what you said about sticking around?"

"You couldn't get rid of me if you tried," he said with a smile, realizing how nice it was to be home with his family. He wanted to see the others now too. And the stranded traveler. It struck him as odd that he couldn't seem to get her out of his mind, considering he'd known her a short time. Even on the drive over he wondered more than once if she'd found a place to settle for the night. She stated she wouldn't be in town long. Would he run into her again?

Tucking away those thoughts as unproductive, he turned to Adam.

"Eric gave me the high level of recent events," he said. "Sorry I missed the Marshall's funeral."

"You didn't," Adam said. "He didn't want anyone making a fuss. All we've had so far is a reading of his will and none of the grandchildren were invited. He requested the family lawyer say a few words before sprinkling his ashes off the bluff. To be honest, it's been too busy around here for everyone to agree on a time for that to happen, and our father and Uncle Keif have never fought more. Plus, I think none of us felt too right about doing it without everyone home. Now, as you probably know, our father is in the hospital."

"Eric said he had a heart attack," Fallon stated.

Adam nodded. "They've been keeping him for observation but I believe he'll be released tomorrow morning."

"That's good to hear," Fallon said.

"Have you spoken to him at all? Are the two of you okay?" Adam asked.

"I can't say that I know the man very well," Fallon admitted. "I don't like the fact he's had affairs. Although, I guess I suspected something when I was a kid. Or maybe I just didn't like his personality all that much. I never did care for the way he treated our mother. The woman has been nothing but a saint. Can't say I remember much about him." He shrugged. "Figured we were two very different people and didn't have much to say to one another. Why?"

"Wasn't sure if something had happened to keep you away for so long," Adam admitted.

"To be honest, I always knew I would come back at some point and take my rightful place here. It's probably the reason I decided to go as far away as possible. Try something new. Travel. I needed to get away to find myself if I wasn't a Firebrand. Serving my country makes me feel like I've done something to deserve this place, rather than just have it handed to me because of my name, if that makes any sense."

"When did you get so grown up?" Adam smiled.

Fallon wiggled his eyebrows before taking another sip of coffee.

"I know exactly what you mean," his brother said.

"I heard about Dane." Fallon figured that was the reason for this line of questioning. His brother had refused to come home after being forced to lie about catching his father in an affair.

Adam's cell buzzed. He checked the screen before responding to a text.

"We have a visitor," Adam said. "Someone who says she has official business and would like to see whoever is in charge."

"Oh, yeah? Does this person have a name?" Fallon picked up on the pronoun. Could it be her?

"Birdie West," Adam supplied.

Fallon's chest fisted.

"You know her?" Adam asked, arching an eyebrow.

"Not really. I just helped her out of a ditch."

The thought of seeing Birdie again stirred something deep in his chest. It wasn't like they'd spent a whole lot of time together, and yet everything about her felt different, special, like she was supposed to be in his life. The strange thought needed to stay shelved for now. Especially since she seemed to have some kind of business with his family.

"Well, she's about to knock on the front door," Adam stated. "After everything that's been going on at the ranch, a few less surprises would be a nice change of pace."

4

Birdie stood on the porch of a two-story brick and stone house that was about the grandest thing she'd ever seen. The front lawn looked more like it belonged on a golf course. She'd noted a set of impressive twin barns behind the house as she'd driven up to the parking area. The fact a residence had a parking area should have been her first clue these folks were beyond loaded with cash. Then again, someone who had a million dollars to give away wasn't the type of person she knew on a personal basis.

Of course, people who had money liked to keep it. Anyone who could afford a home like this one would have access to endless lawyers too. Birdie released the breath she'd been holding, allowing her chest to deflate and her shoulders to round forward. She stared at the doorbell, thinking it was now or never.

Birdie jabbed her index finger into the round circle, causing a set of pipes to sound on the other side of the door.

This would turn out fine. She could handle herself. If the others were like Fallon Firebrand, they would honor their grandfather's wishes. She reminded herself to be strong and confident when she dealt with the family. Confidence was half the battle.

The door opened and a woman with the most sincere set of cobalt blue eyes answered. She cradled a baby in one arm as she swung the door wide open with her free hand. "Hi, I'm Prudence. Come on in."

Birdie stood there for a long moment, blinking. This warm welcome was not what she was expecting. She tucked the folder a little tighter underneath her arm, and stepped inside the massive doorway. The three feet tall palomino horse sculpture sitting on a table to her right caused her chest to squeeze. She would recognize Meg's work anywhere.

"I'm Birdie," she said, finally finding her voice.

"Welcome," Prudence said.

"Is that your daughter?" Birdie asking, thinking that was probably a stupid question but she was trying to make small talk. She'd never been good at it much, preferring to spend a Friday night after a long week at home, soaking in the tub with a glass of wine and a good book. Ethan had pointed out what a buzz-kill she was because they lived near Austin and he wanted to hit the clubs. To be fair, it was exactly what people their age did. Meg had always called Birdie an old soul. Her grandmother hit the nail on the head there.

"This is Angel," Prudence said with a smile that beamed. "And, yes, she's my daughter."

"Her name suits her," Birdie said. She wasn't one for kids in general but this one tugged at her heart.

Before Prudence had a chance to shut the door, Bronc rode up on a golf cart. A Labrador retriever sat next to him.

"That's Hutch," Prudence pointed as the dog came toward them gunning at full speed. "And the little one is Miss Peabody."

Birdie squatted down to greet Hutch. Big mistake as he bowled her over and headed straight for the voice that floated down the hallway. She was knocked onto her backside. Her hands came back to break her fall, landing hard against the unforgiving tile. Her folder went flying. Papers scattered like they'd been caught up in a dust storm. And then a little dog trotted inside, stopping long enough to tinkle on one of the pages.

"Miss Peabody...no." Prudence shooed the little dog away. A few strands of hair escaped her ponytail, landing into her eyes. She blew out a puff of air and must have apologized ten times. "Let me help you."

"I got it," Birdie said, suddenly embarrassed at coming here in the first place. Maybe she should have gone through a lawyer, except that she figured a personal appeal would be best under the circumstances. Meg needed the money now, not in three to five years or however long a court battle could take.

"Birdie?" Fallon's voice traveled over her and through her, warming her in places she needed to ignore. She'd recognize that deep baritone anywhere. "What are you doing here?"

"I have business with the family," she stated, trying to gather her papers and her dignity in one fell swoop. She highly doubted she was succeeding.

"Hutch knocked her down," Prudence said to a second person who'd joined them. He was tall, much like Fallon, and the family resemblance was unmistakable. This must be one of his brothers.

"I'm Adam," he said, kneeling down to catch an errant page. "I'd offer to shake your hand, but you look preoccupied."

Fallon was already on one knee gathering pages. Part of

her wanted to throw her body over the scattered legal document to shield the contents. Meg had said the document needed to be kept in pristine condition to be defensible in court. Thankfully, this was only a copy. The brilliance of her decision not to bring the original shined through. Last she'd checked, dog pee didn't qualify as being in perfect shape.

Birdie caught herself glancing at the statue while thinking of Meg. Seeing her grandmother's work connected them in a sense.

Birdie managed to gather up most of the papers with the ever-present fear she'd just blown Meg's chances at getting what had been promised to her. Fallon handed over a couple of sheets. The pee-stained page stared at them both. With her index finger and thumb, she carefully picked it up, holding it as far away from the others as she could manage, and shook. A yellow line streaked the page as it rolled down.

"I'm so sorry," Prudence said with a mortified look on her face. "Miss Peabody is normally such a good girl."

Adam excused himself before disappearing down the hallway. He rushed back with a handful of paper towels.

"It's okay," Birdie said. Her first impression of the family was good. Fallon had already helped her out of a ditch without expecting anything in return. Granted, she'd taken off pretty fast once she found out he was a Firebrand. But he seemed like a genuinely good person. Meg had warned Birdie about Marshall's sons. She'd said they wouldn't be too happy to know their father had had an affair with an artist. One that had started years ago, and had been on-again, off-again until a few years ago when Marshall stopped reaching out.

Meg hadn't known Marshall was married when they first met. She found out years later after his wife had passed away. Once his wife was gone, Meg didn't see the harm in continuing. It wasn't like they saw each other all the time. They'd become shelters in the storm for each other at different times in their lives. While Meg was married, she stopped the fling. If Marshall dated someone seriously, the same. Each respected the other's relationships. Each reached out when life got too much, or one became too lonely. If the other was available, they spent time together.

Birdie had been floored by the admission. She'd never once heard of or met Marshall Firebrand despite growing up in Texas. To be fair, she didn't hang around in ranching circles. And Meg kept her cards close to her chest where the men in her life were concerned. Except, of course, Christopher. Had Meg been too embarrassed to reach out to Marshall after losing all her money to a liar?

After Ethan, Birdie was convinced Meg had had the right idea with Marshall. No real commitment. Each one led different lives, only coming together when they wanted to. Traditional marriage and family had lost its appeal after the devastating breakup.

But then, had she really seen herself living out the rest of her life with Ethan? Three years had seemed like a long time to be together without taking the next step, though. It seemed like they were supposed to get engaged, then married.

What had her heart wanted? A little voice in the back of her mind said she would have wanted someone like Fallon. The admission shocked her. She chalked it up to the thought of losing Meg. The notion probably had her wanting to grab hold of someone rather than lose everyone she loved. The spark between them was nothing more than good chemistry that could result in hot sex. It couldn't be real or lasting between strangers. Could it?

Fallon ignored the way his pulse raced this close to Birdie. He told himself it was nothing more than feeling good about seeing her again, and knowing she was fine. She'd been fine when she pulled away from him. And yet, something told him that she was treading water, trying to keep her head up.

Did this document have something to do with the reason why? He glanced at the pee-stained page but couldn't make out the words at this angle. She shoved the rest of the pages inside a folder pretty darn quick.

Adam finished cleaning up the tile as Prudence excused herself before taking the baby back inside the playroom.

"Since when did the Marshall get dogs?" Fallon asked his brother.

"They're ours. Long story," Adam said. "Remind me to tell you all about it later."

A lab came gunning down the hallway toward them. On instinct, Fallon pulled Birdie up to standing before the dog could bowl her over again. She stumbled and they ended up body-to-body. He ignored the electrical current pulsing from every point of contact. And there were many.

"Hutch," Prudence called calmly. "Here, boy."

The big dog loped into the playroom.

"We need a gate," Adam said, herding them both inside.

"There's coffee in the kitchen," Fallon said to Birdie as she righted herself. Her cheeks flushed, making her even more beautiful. She was all of five-feet-five-inches with creamy skin and just the right amount of curves that had felt a little too good pressed against his body.

Fallon did his best to shake it off.

"Coffee's good," she said. When she looked up at him,

her autumn eyes glittered with something that looked a whole lot like need.

"Okay. Coffee it is." His vocabulary and speaking ability suddenly resembled that of a high schooler's. His body was having a similar reaction, sweaty palms and a frog in his throat. Fallon would laugh if it was funny. As it was, he'd retreated to a phase in his life when he was all hormones and little brains. "This way."

He needed to get a handle on the attraction, and he would. Being around Birdie was a temporary situation anyway. But he had to say as caught off guard as he was at his reaction to her, it was refreshing to be near someone who affected him. It had been far too long since he'd been around a person who threw him off his game. He'd dated women from around the world while overseas. He'd traveled on leave and had relationships, if they could be called that. They'd always been short-term to his thinking. He was honest about his intentions, or lack thereof. And yet, something had been missing in his life for the past few years. He'd had all the excitement he could handle in his job. And yet, life had taken on a dullness that he couldn't quite place. He figured he was losing his edge and decided not to re-up when it was contract time. Plus, with everything going on at home, he figured it was time.

Fallon fixed a cup of coffee and handed it over to Birdie. "Mind if I ask what business you have with my family?"

"Are you the representative for them?" she asked, guarding the papers like they were made of gold.

He chuckled, and figured it wasn't helping matters.

"I've been back in town all of," he checked the time, "about two hours."

"Oh, right. Thank you again for helping me on the road," she said before taking a sip of coffee. She made a little mewl of pleasure and he wondered if she even realized she'd done it.

It was sexy as all get out.

"No problem. It's what we do in these parts," he said. "At least, it was when I grew up around here. I don't imagine that much has changed."

"You say that like anyone would be willing to stop their life and help a stranger," she said.

"If that isn't what it's like where you're from, you should think about moving," he stated. "But, if you're looking for someone in charge, that would probably be my brother Adam."

"Did someone say my name?" Adam walked into the kitchen.

"I'm Birdie West and I'm here on behalf of my M—" She flashed eyes at Fallon. "Grandmother."

"Okay," Adam said, retrieving his coffee cup. "Is there something I can help you and your grandmother with?"

"I'm not sure. Meg...that's what I call her, said I should come here and ask to speak to whoever has taken over for Marshall Firebrand," she said, shifting her weight from one foot to the other, a sign she was nervous.

Eric had warned Fallon that some folks were honing in on the ranch. Sharks were circling, looking for an easy kill now that the Marshall was gone. Was Birdie one of them?

Fallon didn't want to believe it but that was probably because she was the first interesting person he'd come across in far too long. He studied her, looking for any signs her claws were out. He'd noticed how often she'd glanced at the palomino sculpture the Marshall had commissioned more than twenty years ago. And yet, the label 'gold digger' didn't seem to fit Autumn Eyes. She could be a decoy. She could have been sent to throw the family off while someone plotted another attack.

"That depends on what this is about," Adam continued. "If it has anything to do with the cattle or the land, that would be my side of the family's department. But if it has to do with mineral rights, you'll need to speak to my uncle. Does that help you at all?"

"Not really." She frowned.

"I'm afraid I don't understand what you need, which means I can't help if you don't provide a few more details," Adam said.

"It's about an inheritance." She set a file folder down on the granite island. "Your grandfather left Meg some money."

"Oh? Is that so? Then you'll probably want to have your lawyer send the file to our family's attorney so he can examine it," Adam said.

"She was specific about dealing with the family directly," she said. "Said you might want to keep this confidential."

"Why would..."

Adam stopped mid-sentence. It seemed to dawn on him why someone would want to keep a lid on money being left to a female who wasn't a family member. He set down his coffee and threw his hands in the air. "I'm out of my league here."

"What if we called a family meeting on our side?" Fallon asked. He studied Birdie. Call him naïve but he believed she was an honest person. Could he trust her?

5

"I apologize if I'm throwing everyone for a loop," Birdie started as she looked into Fallon's eyes then Adam's. She far preferred staring into Fallon's but an attraction was out of place, and probably unwelcome considering she was about to tell the honorable Firebrand family that their grandfather had been having an affair since before Birdie was born. "I just learned about all this myself two days ago. Meg...my grandmother handed me a document and said I should bring it to your family."

"Are you saying what I think you are?" Adam's voice was laced with surprise, but she didn't detect a hint of judgment. He probably should have been more shocked than he was.

"Yes," she confirmed.

"For how long?" Adam asked.

She waited for Fallon to jump in and say something but he stayed quiet. He seemed to be observing, withholding judgment.

"A very long time," she said.

"Well, the Marshall seems to be full of surprises," Adam said quietly. There was a hint of disdain in his voice. He walked over to the granite island and motioned toward the papers. "Mind if I take a closer look at these?"

Birdie shook her head, wishing Fallon would speak up.

"You can look all you want, but they leave when I do," Birdie said. She had to be firm on that point.

"I'll need to run this past the family lawyer," Adam stated, and it dawned on her that he would need to validate the document in some way. She probably should have thought of it before.

"How do you plan to do that?" she asked.

"Our attorney's name is Harlen Sawyer," Adam supplied. "He can get in touch with your attorney."

Birdie's pulse kicked up a few notches as she realized how unprepared for this meeting she really was.

"So...Meg doesn't have a lawyer," Birdie said.

"Mind if I take a picture of a couple of the pages?" Adam asked.

Was he already trying to figure a way out of parting with the money? Trying to find a reason to dismiss the claim?

"Go ahead," she said, figuring he had to see the details at some point. "I don't know if this matters to either of you, but Meg has been holding onto this will for a long time. I wouldn't be here if she didn't need the money."

"No offense to you or your Meg, but we can't take someone's word when it comes to what sounds like might be a large sum of money," Adam stated. "People would be crawling out of the woodwork to get a piece of our family's legacy."

"Oh, right. I understand," she said, figuring he'd just called her a liar. She panicked and her gaze immediately searched for the back door.

"My brother isn't saying that he doesn't believe you," Fallon finally spoke up, and she realized he'd been lowkey studying the interaction the whole time. There he was, throwing her a lifeline again. "He's only saying that he wants to ensure this is a legitimate claim before bringing it to our family's attention or acting on it."

"It is," she defended. "Meg wouldn't lie about something so personal."

Fallon gave a slight nod.

She also realized how defensive that must have sounded, but it was true.

"Why come here? Why not just contact our family lawyer?" Fallon asked. She must have shot him a look because he added, "I'm just playing catch up here. Trying to better understand this situation."

"For one, Meg is hoping to avoid a big ordeal. Secondly, if details of the affair get out it could damage your grandfather's reputation. She'd rather not get a dime if it meant making Marshall look bad or bringing a stain on the family name." She stopped herself right there. "This isn't a threat, by the way. This is Meg requesting Marshall's wishes be honored."

"This predates the current will," Adam said after examining the pages.

"I'm no lawyer but wouldn't the current will have some language in there to cancel out anything that came before it?" Fallon asked.

"That's the idea," Adam confirmed. "But that doesn't mean there isn't a clause in the current one. I don't know why those details wouldn't have been shared with us already. Maybe Meg had to come forward to claim it." Adam studied the document like he was sequencing genes that had the answer to curing childhood diseases like smallpox.

"Hold on a second. What is this?" Adam asked, his eyebrow shooting up.

"What's going on, Adam?" Fallon asked, moving next to his brother.

"This document gives everything to us," Adam stated in disbelief.

"Come again," Fallon said, a little louder this time.

Adam pointed as Birdie took a step away before she accidentally made physical contact with Fallon again. She needed a clear mind if she was going to stand her ground. And yet, she couldn't help but think she'd just delivered the shock of the century. Surprisingly enough, she didn't think it had anything to do with Meg.

"This will is dated four years ago. The current one is from last year." Adam stood tall and scratched his head. "That basically means the Marshall changed his mind about how he planned to split this place last year."

"Unless there's another will out there somewhere from the years in between," Fallon pointed out.

"That could be true. Not sure about the odds, though. Either way, this is huge," Adam stated.

All Birdie heard was this whole situation blowing up in Meg's face. If this document changed the state of all the inheritance, there could be a lengthy court battle from within the family. All hopes this could be cleared up in a matter of days shriveled on the vine. All hopes that Meg would get the money she needed for her care died. All hopes for a last-minute save canceled.

"We need an immediate family meeting," Adam said. "This changes everything."

"Why?" Fallon asked. "You're going to have to give me more than a statement like that if you want me to understand."

"Because someone might have coerced the Marshall into changing his will and that leaves a legal door wide open to contest the current one," Adam stated. He held up a finger. "Hold on a second."

Fallon's forehead wrinkled with confusion.

"Stay with me for a minute." Adam disappeared down the hall, returning a few minutes later. He spread a document out on the granite island. "I'm not seeing it, are you?"

Birdie finished her cup of coffee, figuring she'd better come up with a different plan to help Meg. At the moment, plans to successfully deliver the will and get a commitment for the payout seemed to be failing miserably.

"What are we looking for exactly?" Fallon asked.

"The clause you mentioned. It should start the will," Adam said. "We need to give these to our family lawyer, but a case can be made that all the mineral rights, cattle, and land belong to our side of the family."

"I hear what you're suggesting but that's a powder keg if ever I've heard one," Fallon stated. "Considering the state our family has been in this summer, this might be providing the spark."

"Aunt Jackie tried to get close with the Marshall in his last couple of years," Adam said. "I never have trusted that woman. What if she manipulated him into changing the will?"

"The Marshall?" Fallon scoffed. "I can't imagine anyone could make him do something he didn't want to do."

"As difficult as it is to believe, he was getting up there in years," Adam stated. "Of course, our uncle or any one of our cousins could have been involved, especially if Aunt Jackie thought she'd learned something."

Birdie watched the exchange. Much to her horror, it sounded like Meg had just given the family something to fight about. Of course, if this will was validated, there was no denying Meg the money. But how long would that take? Months? Years? *Too long.*

FALLON FOUND himself in the position of wanting to help Birdie out for a second time. He'd seen her face turn bleach-sheet white as Adam cranked up his argument. But shouldn't she be happy that he wanted to validate her grandmother's version of the will? Why did she look like she'd just bet her rent money on a losing horse?

"I better go," Birdie said, her gaze darting around, looking for the quickest exit. He'd seen the same expression earlier at the ditch. "You should take your pictures now."

"Are you staying in town tonight?" Fallon asked, taking what might be his only chance to intervene. He'd never received a clear answer from her earlier and it dawned on him that she might not have a place. He wasn't the type to judge others but her vehicle was old and he wondered just how tight she might be on funds.

"Not really," she said, non-committal.

"Do you need a place?" he asked, then added, "Don't get the wrong idea. I'm not hitting on you. I just realized that you're visiting and there isn't a decent place to stay this far outside of town."

Her cheeks flushed, and he realized he'd hit the jackpot.

"I'll be okay," she said.

"Are you sure? Because it's no trouble," he continued, feeling his way through this conversation. "I have a place on property with a nice guest room if you're interested. It's free and you'd be doing me a favor by staying there."

"Oh, I mean, if it's not any trouble. It's already dark outside, so I could probably stay even though I already paid for a night." She shifted her weight from foot to foot again, her telltale sign of being nervous.

"I haven't been home in years. I have no idea what we'd be getting ourselves into, but I'm game if you are," he said, figuring he needed to get her out of the main house before Adam scared her off property for good. "I'd be happy to reimburse you."

"Sure." She shrugged her shoulders nonchalant, but he could tell it was a very big deal to her that she'd just agreed to spend the night at a virtual stranger's home. She glanced at the papers that Adam was currently snapping pics of.

"Almost done there?" Fallon asked his brother.

"One more," Adam said. He seemed to have locked onto the new will a little too intensely for Birdie's comfort. But then everything about her body language said she was out of her comfort zone. A liar? Was this a fabricated will? Fallon considered himself good at reading people and Birdie seemed like the real deal to him.

"We're about to head out, so we're going to need those," Fallon said to Adam.

"Okay." He snapped the final pic. "All done."

Fallon caught his brother's gaze and held it. "Promise me that you won't stir up trouble until we have a chance to talk to Mom, Dad, and the lawyer about this."

"I'll do what I can," Adam promised. His brother's word was as good as gold. But, yeah, news like this was going to be hard to keep under the radar.

"Thanks. I'll see you tomorrow morning," Fallon said.

Adam cocked an eyebrow. Their conversation from earlier must have dawned on him.

"We'll catch up later," was all Fallon said by way of explanation. "I'll walk Birdie out."

She couldn't gather up the document fast enough. The

discovery seemed to have rattled her. Fallon wanted to get to the bottom of why before news leaked.

"Do you want to follow me to my place?" he asked.

"Okay." There was a whole lot going on behind those big eyes of hers. Too bad he couldn't figure out what because he had no idea what to say to help. She was intelligent and strong. He had to trust she would speak up when she was ready. All he could do was make her feel safe around him.

He hopped into his truck, and then made the twenty-minute drive to his lakeside cabin. Birdie parked beside him. He noticed a pillow and blanket on the passenger side. She grabbed an overnight bag from her backseat while he made a move to unlock the front door. Either she traveled with her own bedding, which was highly unlikely, or she'd planned to sleep in her vehicle. In this heat, that could be dangerous. Fallon felt even better about following his instincts to invite her to his home.

Home? It was difficult to view this cabin as home considering he'd never spent a night here. He'd overseen the plans. He'd picked out the finishes. He'd seen the construction through, figuring someday he would come back and claim the place. Family events pushed his timeline. He couldn't deny having another person with him to walk through the front door eased the tension that had been forming knots in his shoulder blades.

The sun had disappeared long ago. It was getting late, and Fallon realized he should have done more than drink coffee while at Adam's. He should have borrowed a few supplies while he'd been at the main house. Fallon stepped inside the living room and flipped on a light. His stomach picked that moment to growl, which happened to coincide with Birdie's entrance.

"I have a power bar in here." She motioned toward her bag.

"Thanks. I may have to take you up on that." Was that how she'd planned to survive while in Lone Star Pass? Eating power bars and, what, sleeping in her car? He really was glad that she'd agreed to stay at his place.

"Wow," Birdie said as she glanced around.

"I'm going to be honest, I'd expected to walk in to sheets covering the furniture and inch thick dust on the fireplace mantle." Much to his surprise, the house was clean. Right. Eric knew Fallon was coming home today. Was his brother responsible for making sure Fallon's place was livable? He owed Eric a thank you. Knowing Eric, he would have seen to it that everything was stocked.

"Lucky you," she said, "I'm the one who cleans at Meg's."

"Make yourself at home," Fallon said. He motioned toward a stairwell that led upstairs. "There's a guest bedroom to the right of the loft."

Chin up, she took a couple of steps in a circle while seeming to take in the expansive open-concept home. "This place is beautiful."

"Thank you," he said, and meant it. The home didn't look big from the outside, which was done on purpose. The inside was deceptively large, mainly because it was so open. High ceilings helped. The living space had a leather sofa, loveseat, and pair of matching chairs. The ground floor was covered in light-colored tile. An open second floor loft gave the space an expansive feel. Pine paneling throughout lightened the wall and gave the authentic cabin feel that had been important to Fallon. A large rectangle dining table could easily hold eight in the event that a few of his brothers came over. Upstairs had a card table, a pool table, and a flat-screen mounted to the wall. He'd built a place for entertaining and then moved as far away as he could. The irony was not lost on him.

"Did you do all this?" She blinked a couple of times in what looked like amazement. His chest filled with something that felt a lot like pride.

"I called our resident expert to help pick out furnishings," he admitted. "So, I can't take full credit. I just told my mother what I envisioned for my home, and the right furniture showed up."

"Still, I'm impressed," she said, and his heart swelled with pride.

Despite designing the layout and picking everything out during the two-year project from eighteen to twenty, he would make the same choices today. Fallon had always had a strong sense of what he liked, and what he wanted. His tastes hadn't changed much over the years. He still appreciated simple things over flashy ones, and substance over style.

His stomach growled again, reminding him of the need to find food fast before he became hungry enough to bite his own arm off. He took a chance on the fridge, opening it to find it stocked.

"My brother Eric seems to have made certain there was plenty of food in the fridge." With his mother staying at the hospital twenty-four-seven, the food containers had to be the work of Miss Olive, the Marshall's housekeeper. The woman was an amazing cook.

"Are you hungry?" Fallon asked Birdie as she made her way up the stairs.

"A little," she said.

"How do you feel about sour cream chicken enchiladas?" he asked.

"Is that a serious question?" she shot back with the sound of enthusiasm in her voice.

"Enchiladas it is," he said, pulling out a container of what would be some of the best food he'd had in longer than he cared to remember. He'd had to block out most of the good in his past in order to keep his head in the game while in the military. Otherwise, he would have tapped out when his first tour was up and returned to the comforts of home. Being sixth in a family of nine boys had made him want to prove himself.

The smell filled the kitchen even before the microwave beeped. His stomach growled again as Birdie came downstairs. He filled two plates. "Take a seat anywhere you like."

Birdie chose a spot nearest the wall of windows overlooking the lake. "It's so beautiful here."

He nodded as he set the table.

"Why would anyone ever leave a place like this?" she asked low and under her breath.

"A whole lot of reasons," he answered despite the fact she'd probably asked a rhetorical question.

"Name one," she said. "But also, can I help you with anything?"

He shook his head as he set the plates down. He retrieved a couple glasses and filled them with water before joining her at the table.

"This looks and smells amazing," she said, those expressive eyes taking it all in.

"Independence," he stated.

She shot a confused look at him.

"It's easy to lose your identity when you grow up in a large and famous cattle ranching family," Fallon said.

"I've only been here an hour or two and I already think I understand what that might do to a person." Birdie took a bite of food, and then mewled with pleasure. "Okay, this is amazing."

He smiled.

"Get used to this and you start thinking life is supposed to be this," he said. "Suddenly, you don't know who you are if 'this' is taken away."

6

Birdie sat looking out the window after they finished eating. Fallon's words cycled through her thoughts. The part about getting used to something and then expecting it resonated.

"I think I have an understanding of what you mean," she finally said.

"About?" He brought over two cups of coffee, then hot apple pie for dessert.

"This." She motioned toward the table.

He reclaimed his seat but his eyebrow shot up.

"Does food show up every time you need a full fridge?" She wanted to confirm she was on the right track.

"Exactly," he said. "Granted, my parents instilled a work ethic in all of us that most folks will never have and I'll go to my grave appreciating them for it."

"But you also didn't have to lift a finger for there to be food on the table every night," she added.

"That's right. Ranching was all I knew. The ranching way of life, as much as it's a part of me, was so ingrained in me that I didn't know who I was outside of it," he said. "Then, there was the financial inheritance."

"Money that you didn't earn." She cocked her head to the side as she listened. She wanted to understand his line of thinking because she'd grown up believing it was a magic ticket to happiness.

"Or do anything to deserve," he said.

"So you went into the service in order to pay it back?" That part she wasn't too clear on.

"To deserve it," he said. "I was born into all this and I needed to earn my place."

She nodded as he studied her.

"Does that make sense?" he asked.

"In a way, yes," she admitted. "I also understand about not getting too comfortable."

"What if I lost everything?" he continued, and the way his eyes lit up she could tell that she'd struck a chord. "I needed to know that I could start from nothing and rebuild."

"And the military did that for you?" she asked.

"It was hard in the beginning. Harder than I ever thought it would be," he said before taking a sip of coffee. "The whole point of basic training is to strip you down so you can be rebuilt. I went in cocky because I knew a hard day's work. I wasn't worried about the physical aspect. But I learned very quickly my mental game needed the attention."

"I used to hate camping," she said, nodding. The comment elicited a raised eyebrow. "The sounds used to scare me, and Texas is usually too hot or too cold. There's not a whole lot of middle ground. But then, one night I really listened. The crickets chirping were kind of musical. They became a lullaby. Now, all I have to do when I can't sleep is turn on 'outdoor sounds'. I'm out in less than a minute."

"That's exactly it. It's a different game when you realize that you can overcome any obstacle without anyone else's help," he stated. "I needed to figure that out, and that's what being in the military gave me."

"That's amazing." She thought about Meg, who'd made something of herself and then lost it all. How her health seemed to decline not too long after. And how the past couple of years her spirit soon followed. The mind and heart were powerful.

The last thing Birdie wanted to do now was let Meg down. She wouldn't be able to survive it. In her younger years, this would be a different story. Meg was fragile now.

Birdie feared the will would stir up a whole bunch of controversy within the family. So much so, she was kind of surprised Fallon was being so nice. Was he being genuine? Or feeling out the enemy?

Logic said it would be a smart move on his behalf. Although, he could have left her on the side of the road and didn't. Of course, that was before he found out why she was really here. Did he regret his actions? She was reminded of the old saying, *keep your friends close and your enemies closer.*

Her heart argued against the idea. And since it had been right about Ethan when she'd felt him distancing himself from her, she decided to pay attention to it.

"Beautiful view," she said, purposely changing the subject. Every time the man looked at her, her heart skipped a few beats and her stomach free fell. The physical reaction she had to him caught her off guard. She would get up and out early in the morning before he woke up. Getting to know him better would do no good. Being here wouldn't do any good. Besides, based on his brother Adam's reaction to the will and the complication of it changing everything for the family, there would be a long legal fight. Even if Meg got the money Marshall Firebrand had intended to leave her at one time, it would come too late.

Birdie had no use for other people's money, so she wouldn't go after it on her own. She was still young enough to work and make her way in life. Had the medical bills set her back? Yes, of course. But not so much she couldn't pick herself up again.

Right now, she needed to figure out a way to keep enough money coming in to afford Meg's medication, food, and keep a roof over their heads.

"Everything okay?" Fallon's deep timbre traveled over her and through her, shocking her out of her heavy thoughts.

"Yeah," she said quickly. Too quickly. She tried to cover by taking a sip of coffee. As much as she felt comforted by Fallon's presence, she also realized she needed to move on. "I'm stuffed. I should probably take a shower and wind down."

"Okay," he said. "I'm guessing my brother made sure the rooms were all set, including the bathrooms. Holler down if there's anything you need."

"Thank you. For everything today." Before her mind could snap to an attraction place it didn't need to go with Fallon, she excused herself, took her plate and cup to the sink, and then headed upstairs.

The shower was warm, the bath towel fuzzy, and the comforter soft. She set her cell phone alarm and then plugged her phone in to recharge the battery. When sleep seemed nowhere close after half an hour of tossing and turning, she put on 'outdoor sounds', and fell into a deep sleep.

Her alarm went off at five o'clock in the morning. Birdie shot straight up out of bed and glanced around, trying to orient herself. She was in Fallon Firebrand's guest room on the Firebrand family ranch. If someone would have told her yesterday at this time that this was going to happen, she would have said they had no idea what they were talking about.

The will changed everything for this family. The trip was a bust. The time to cut her losses and figure out Plan B had come.

Without making so much as a sound, Birdie collected her things, packed her bag, and then headed downstairs. Halfway down, a stair creaked. She froze, not wanting to wake Fallon. He'd just returned home after many years of being out of the picture and away from his family. She respected him even more now that she knew the reasons why. But that respect was dangerous to her heart—a heart that didn't need to be stomped on twice in the same year.

The realization struck her as odd. She barely knew Fallon, despite feeling like they were twin souls. Feelings could be deceiving, though. There had been a time when she'd trusted Ethan, too. A small voice in the back of her mind tried to argue the two situations couldn't be more different. The voice also pointed out the fact she'd never felt this strong stir of attraction for her ex.

Either way, she was out of here in less than two minutes. She hadn't seen an alarm system or heard Fallon disarm or arm one, so slipping out the front door shouldn't be a big problem. One thing she'd always noticed about living in the country with Meg was how dark it always got inside and out.

Walking slowly, feeling her way with her hand against the wall, she moved toward where she remembered the front door to be. The smell of coffee assaulted her, practically causing her mouth to water. It must be left over from last night. Right? Or maybe her desire was *that* strong and she just *wanted* a cup to be waiting in the kitchen.

With her hand on the door handle, a light flipped on in the kitchen.

"Hey," Fallon's early morning sleepy voice caused all kinds of sensations to travel over her body.

"Um, hi," she said lamely. She turned around to face him, and her heart took another hit. He stood there, shirtless, with muscles for days and a disappointed look on his face. "I didn't think you'd be up this early and I didn't want to disturb you, so I packed up and figured I'd get back on the road before sunlight. I hope it's okay with you and not rude because I was only trying to give you space and be polite."

She was rambling, a sure sign she felt guilty.

"You're not being held against your will here," Fallon said. There was a whole lot of defensiveness in his tone that he needed to rein in. Whether Birdie West stuck around or not was entirely up to her. "I do have one question, though. If you don't mind my asking."

"Go for it." Birdie shrugged, looking a little too beautiful in those shorts and boots this early in the morning.

"You drove a long way to get here. Did you get what you came for?" he asked.

"No, I didn't," she said with the most refreshing honesty.

"Then, can I ask why you're leaving?"

"Your one question is up," Birdie said, then turned and walked out the door.

Fallon fought the temptation to follow her. Instead, he

picked up his cell phone and made the call to Eric. His brother should be up by now and deserved a thank you plus an update on what was most likely going to go down today with the new will.

Eric picked up on the first ring at the same time a blood-curdling scream sounded outside.

"Let me call you right back," Fallon said before setting his phone on the counter and bolting toward the front door. As he reached for the knob, a second scream cut through the air. Fallon practically ripped the door off its hinges.

"Ohmygod. Ohmygod." Birdie stood a good fifteen feet away from the driver's side of her vehicle, her hands clasped at her chest. She glanced up at him and it was like a bomb detonated inside his chest. "Snake. It rattled. I got out of there."

"A rattlesnake inside your vehicle?" Fallon had no plans to climb inside her hatchback to investigate.

"Yes. I saw it. It rattled at me. I panicked and got the heck out of there."

He didn't want to think news of the new will had leaked, or that someone on the other side of the family had done something so cruel and dangerous. Birdie could have been killed if she'd been struck.

First things first, he needed to confirm there was, in fact, a rattlesnake in her vehicle before he got too worked up. It was a sad state when there was a danger present and his first thought was that the other side of the family had done something wrong. As proved recently, others were interested in trying to take his family down in what they saw as a vulnerable time for the Firebrands. There were most likely more that would climb out of the woodwork.

Given Eric's update, everyone needed to stay alert. Speaking of his brother, he decided to call him back. In fact, if someone truly was trying to hurt someone on the ranch, Sheriff Lawler would need to be involved. A rattlesnake couldn't easily get inside someone's vehicle. One would be more likely to be found on the porch as the sun came up.

"Did you lock your doors last night?" Fallon asked.

"No, I didn't," she admitted. "I didn't think I would need to."

"Walk me through exactly what happened," he said, keeping a safe distance from the vehicle.

"I walked over here to Blue Jay, and then opened the door." Panic widened her eyes at the memory. "I tossed my bag onto the passenger side and sat down. Then, I saw something move in the floorboard at the same time I heard the rattle. I hopped out of there so fast it would make your head spin. At some point I screamed a couple of times, but I seriously don't remember all that much about that part."

"So you touched the handle on the driver's side only?" he asked.

Birdie cocked her head to one side as realization seemed to dawn. "You don't think this is an accident, do you?"

"To be honest, I have no idea," he said. "But I'm not willing to take a chance, either. Not after all that's been happening lately and everything that's at stake."

Birdie nodded and took another step back.

"It was a mistake to come here," she said. "I should have realized something like this might have happened."

"You're fine," he said. "You followed your grandmother's wishes. I didn't know the Marshall very well but if he wanted your grandmother to have something, we wouldn't have a problem respecting his wishes."

"I stirred up a hornet's nest," she said, shaking her head.

Was that why she'd tried to sneak out this morning? She was afraid of the backlash?

"It's too late for this to be undone," he stated. "But hold on right there. I need to grab my phone, put on my boots, and make a couple of calls."

He waited for her to agree.

"Keep an eye on the vehicle but don't touch anything," he added.

"Okay," she relented, shifting her weight from her right leg to her left. He'd noticed the nervous habit earlier.

Fallon jogged into the house, grabbed his cell, and came back. There was a text waiting from Eric that was three question marks. Fallon called Eric back immediately.

"Hey, strange thing just happened. It's a long story but suffice it to say that we need the sheriff to stop by. It's Lawler, right?" Fallon asked.

"Yes, but what happened?" Eric asked.

"I have a houseguest. On her way out, she found a rattlesnake in her car," Fallon said.

"What in the name of—" Eric seemed to stop himself. "I'll call the sheriff. He keeps rancher hours, so he'll most likely be awake and raring to go."

"Thanks. I'll keep watch on the vehicle until he arrives," Fallon said.

"Everyone is okay, though. Right?" Eric asked.

"We're good." Fallon ended the call after a quick goodbye. He turned to Birdie and said, "I should have asked you first. Do you mind sticking around until the sheriff gets a handle on what might have happened here?"

"There's no chance a rattler just slithered into my car, is there?" she asked, sounding resigned.

Fallon shook his head. For her sake, he wished it was that simple. The unexpected gift was that she would stick around a couple more hours at least. Could he use the time to get answers from her?

7

Birdie had already said enough. From here on out, she intended to keep her mouth closed. Normally, that wasn't a problem for her. She would never be accused of being the chatty type. But with Fallon, she found that she wanted to open up more, wanted to let him in. Since that had worked out so well in her past relationship, she wouldn't go there. Again, an annoying voice tried to point out that Fallon couldn't be more different than Ethan. Plus, her ex did more talking in the relationship. He'd stepped away from pitching in to help run his family's successful furniture store business to be a financial advisor. Fallon was doing the opposite, claiming his birthright after being darn certain it was what he wanted to do and that he'd done something to deserve it.

Ethan, on the other hand, had enjoyed living off his family's money. When his father asked him to pitch in more so he could learn the business, Ethan had balked. He'd complained to Birdie that if he was going to work long hours, it should be for himself and not to make his 'lazy' sisters more money. Birdie hadn't been close enough with

Jennifer and Leslie to know any different. Until she'd over-heard Ethan's father say he wished Ethan would pull his weight instead of depending on his sisters to cover for him all the time. It had been eye-opening. When she'd asked Ethan why his father would say something like that, he'd said that his father didn't appreciate his contributions.

After she was burned by him a few months later, she realized just how many other excuses she'd been making for the man. Never again would she listen to someone's words rather than pay attention to their actions. Ethan, it seemed, had decided financial advising would be a cushy job. As for those long hours at work? Birdie didn't want to envision what he was doing with the intern instead. Thankfully, embarrassment couldn't kill a person or she'd be long gone after the fool he'd made of her. Fallon and Ethan couldn't be more opposite in personality, and just about every other department when she really thought about it. Besides, it was time to close the book where Ethan was concerned.

"There's coffee inside if you'd like to go in and make a cup for yourself." Fallon's voice broke into her heavy thoughts.

"That would be nice, actually," she said, figuring he had as much of an interest in finding out who was responsible for the snake as she did. She shivered thinking about the fact someone might have placed it inside her vehicle. That someone wanted her hurt or worse. Dead?

"Are you okay?" Fallon asked. "You can be honest if you're not."

"I'm shaken up," she said, figuring all she needed to do was get her bearings again. She was also resolved not to let someone intimidate her. "But I'll survive."

She'd been surviving on her own for most of her life. Hold on. Where did that come from?

"Let me know if anything changes and you want to talk about it," he said. "People tell me I'm a good listener."

"I'm a better listener than talker," she admitted, despite the fact talking to Fallon seemed like the most natural thing. "But I'll take you up on that coffee."

"Mind topping off mine? My cup should be on the counter," he said. "We might be out here a minute."

"Not at all." Birdie walked inside the cabin, thinking she'd had the best sleep in longer than she wanted to remember. Ever since Meg's sickness, Birdie never gave herself more than a couple hours of rest at a time. She'd grab as much sleep as possible in between working as a barista at the crack of dawn and then working the dinner shift as a waitress at Barb-e-q, a foodie place out in the country folks came from all over the state to try.

She refilled Fallon's mug before locating a cup for herself and filling it. One sip of the dark roast and the cobwebs started to clear. Of course, finding a rattlesnake in her car had been all the jolt she'd needed. Her heart practically pounded out of her chest.

Glancing at the clock, she realized it was still way too early to call and check on Meg. Birdie had unwittingly stirred a hornet's nest by coming here. She'd gone against her better judgment. Something had warned her this could go very wrong. Of course, she never would have imagined this turn of events. A will that predated the current one that also gave everything to one side of the Firebrand family?

Consider her mind blown.

She'd left the front door cracked so she could finagle it open with the toe of her boot. She kicked it closed behind her as a truck pulled up, practically blinding her with its headlights.

The driver must've caught on because the lights were

dimmed almost immediately but not before she saw stars in her eyes as she exited the porch. She blinked a couple of times and prayed she didn't miss a step or end up with spilled coffee all over her.

Thankfully, neither happened.

"I'll take one of those from you," Fallon said, meeting her halfway. "This should be my brother Eric and his new bride, Romy."

Sure enough, a couple exited the truck that was parked at a safe distance. Romy was taller than Birdie by a good couple of inches. She had hair black as night that fell just past her shoulders in a long wave, the most sincere set of light blue eyes, and a warmth that literally exuded from her smile.

"I'm Romy. It's nice to meet you," she said, offering a handshake.

"Birdie," she said. "Nice to meet you too."

Fallon pulled his brother into a bear of a hug. Eric was built like a tank with arms that resembled bands of steel. His brown hair and green eyes did little to detract from the family resemblance.

"I'm Eric, by the way," his brother said once he and Fallon were done.

"Birdie," she said with another handshake. Having been an only child, she was curious about what it was like to grow up with so many siblings and cousins running around. Birdie's curiosity was piqued. And then there was Eric and Romy to consider. The two genuinely looked in love. And happy. Birdie had never met her father. Her mother had become serious with a couple of men over the years, but he'd always been a mystery.

"Let me show you what's going on," Fallon said to Eric

after offering his brother a cup of coffee. Eric declined, saying he'd already had his caffeine.

"I'm sorry to hear about what happened," Romy said to Birdie. "After what we've been through, I know how scary this is."

"Did you have a similar incident?" Birdie didn't mind the distraction and she needed to feel out if these incidences were connected. Besides, it was still too early to check in with Meg. As it was, all she could do was wait for the sheriff.

Romy gave a quick rundown of her sister ending up pregnant by a prominent businessman who blackmailed Romy into going undercover to spy on the Firebrands. In a matter of a few days, she'd fallen in love with Eric and the family. "My sister is in treatment as we speak, getting the help she needs."

"I'm sorry for what you've been through, but it sounds like it's all turning out well," Birdie said, admiring Romy's strength. From the sounds of it, she'd been through the wringer and back, and came out stronger on the other side.

"Meeting Eric was the best thing that's ever happened to me. My half-sister is getting the help she needs after struggling so much from an abusive childhood. This was one of the most difficult things I've ever been through, but we came out on the other side. And now I have Eric," she said, beaming at the mention of her husband. "I never thought I needed anyone else in my life. And I don't. I mean, I was fine on my own. Finding Eric completed me in a way that's hard to explain."

Birdie had no idea what that was like. Although, since she'd been around Fallon, she was starting to think she might have some idea. Being a whole person, never needing anyone else was a good thing in her book. And yet, she sensed being around Fallon was different. She couldn't explain how because she didn't want to give it a whole lot of consideration.

"Ever since Meg," she flashed eyes at Romy, "that's my grandmother's name."

Romy nodded and smiled.

"Anyway, ever since she became sick, life has changed." Birdie had no idea why she was admitting this to Romy, except to say she'd met another kindred spirit.

"I'm so sorry," Romy said with the kind of compassion that brought a tear to Birdie's eye. "I know how hard it is to see someone you love suffering and feel like there's nothing you can do to help. It's the worst feeling in the world."

Birdie couldn't agree more. She nodded, tucking her chin to her chest to hide the rogue tear that spilled down her cheek.

The sounds of gravel crunching underneath tires broke into the moment. Rays of light were starting to streak the morning sky as the sheriff parked his SUV. He exited his vehicle and then walked over to Birdie's, where Eric and Fallon were standing.

"I'm here if you need someone to talk to," Romy said, reaching out and touching Birdie's arm. "Although, I've heard very good things about my brother-in-law being an amazing listener."

"I might just take you up on that sometime." Birdie liked Romy right away, which was unusual for her. It normally took a whole lot longer for Birdie to feel comfortable around someone. But then, there was something special about being at the Firebrand Ranch that made her feel like she was right at home.

Fallon?

Call Fallon out of his right mind but there was something very right about watching Birdie connect with his sister-in-law. He had yet to get to know Romy but the difference in Eric when he was around her couldn't be ignored. There was something about the way his brother would casually glance over at his new bride at the same moment she looked at him that resonated with Fallon. They were in sync and seemed to communicate without needing words. Not to mention this was the happiest Fallon had ever seen his brother.

"Good morning," the sheriff said as he joined them. Timothy Lawler had been a couple of grades ahead of Adam in school, so the two of them were familiar with each other. Lawler had been a star quarterback who'd been scouted by some big-name programs. A hit that broke his arm in multiple places had ended his football career. He'd gone to school and studied criminal justice instead and then followed in his father's footsteps in law enforcement.

The sheriff was tall but that was where any similarities ended. The man was about as fair-skinned as someone could be. He had ginger hair in a cut that Fallon immediately recognized as military. Other than that, he had a hawk-like nose and compassionate honey-brown eyes. Even on a day that promised to be triple digit temperatures, he wore jeans, boots, and a tan shirt with the word, Sheriff, embroidered on the right front pocket.

"Morning, Sheriff," Eric said. The two shook hands, clearly familiar with each other.

"I hear you just returned from the military," Lawler said to Fallon. "Thank you for your service."

"You're welcome," Fallon said before taking the outstretched hand in a vigorous shake. He introduced Birdie next before the sheriff greeted Romy.

Now that everyone was on the same page, Birdie re-stated what had happened.

"We kept the snake inside the vehicle for proof, but I'm sure it'll make a run for it if we open the door," Fallon said.

"Did anyone besides Miss West touch the driver's side door handle?" Lawler asked.

"Please, call me Birdie," she said. "And I'm the only one who touched it that I know of."

Lawler nodded. He retrieved what Fallon assumed was a fingerprint kit from his vehicle. He methodically moved around the vehicle with some type of a light source that cast an orange glow, stopping to take pictures as he went. "A door handle is generally a good surface to lift fingerprints."

"Sounds encouraging," Birdie said. "Do you need mine for comparison?"

"When you got your license, you were fingerprinted in Texas," Lawler said. "You'll be in the database already."

"Interesting," Birdie said. "How long will it take to process the ones you photographed?"

"A couple of hours at the most," he said before sending the pictures off via text message.

Fallon's information would definitely be in the system, but he wasn't worried about his name coming up as a suspect. He hadn't touched her vehicle. He distinctly remembered going straight to unlock his front door when they'd arrived last night.

"That's fast," Birdie said.

"Let's hope for a hit. If the person is from Texas, there's a good chance the state got a fingerprint from a driver's license application before being told to stop. Those finger-prints were sent to a couple of databases, including the FBI. They used to grab all ten, now it's just a thumb," he informed.

Of course, if no one left a print that could tell them a whole lot about whether or not someone did this as a prank or with intention. He couldn't imagine someone playing a joke like this. It wasn't funny. Despite his family members pulling all kinds of pranks on each other as kids, no one would step this far out of line. A poacher? It was unlikely but not impossible. Why her vehicle though, especially after last night and the will?

The sheriff walked around the perimeter of the vehicle a couple of times, taking pictures from various angles. A few minutes later, he walked over to the group.

"If there's nothing else, I'll head back to my office," he said.

As much as Fallon didn't want to give away the findings in the new will, it could be relevant. Eric would find out sooner or later if this situation was truly escalating. He shot off a quick text to Adam before asking the sheriff to stay another minute.

Fallon glanced at Eric before starting.

"I'd appreciate if the information I'm about to share stays right here in this circle until we're ready to make an announcement," Fallon began.

Eric widened his stance like he was preparing to take a physical punch. He seemed to pick up on the gravity of the announcement Fallon was about to make.

"There's a new will," Fallon said. He glanced at Birdie, who dropped her gaze to the ground. "It predates the current one and changes everything about the inheritance."

"Who stands to benefit from this development?" Lawler asked.

"My side of the family benefits in a huge way," Fallon admitted.

"Who knows about this?" Lawler asked, his eyebrow shot up.

"The people standing in this circle, along with Adam and Prudence as far as I know," Fallon said.

"Is it possible anyone else overheard or got hold of the new will?" Lawler asked.

"I guess so," Fallon said. "Although, I didn't see or hear anyone in the house but us. My brother did take pictures of the will. Birdie still has the document with her."

She also had a death grip on her coffee mug. Her gaze followed the road away from Fallon's house. Why did the fact she was looking for another exit hit him square in the chest?

"Mind if I make a copy of the document?" Lawler asked Birdie. He could get a subpoena, but Fallon figured asking was the easiest way to accomplish the goal.

"It's inside the bag on my passenger side." Birdie, on the other hand, looked ready to climb out of her skin.

8

Birdie hadn't considered how much more complicated her situation just became now that the law was involved. "Um, sure. I guess so."

"The will is inside her bag, so we'll have to wait for her passenger to get out of the vehicle before we can get to it," Fallon said.

"That's right," she stated. "And I'd appreciate not being the one who opens the door."

"I can do it for you," Fallon volunteered.

"We'll help guide it back out there where it belongs," Eric said.

Birdie took a couple more steps away from Blue Jay. "Be my guest."

Romy followed, moving beside Birdie and grabbed her hand. The two clung to each other.

"Can I admit something?" Romy asked.

"Fine by me," Birdie said.

"I hate snakes." A tremor rocked Romy's body.

"Same," was all Birdie said. "You would think that growing up in Texas would make me used to all kinds of creepy crawly critters. But no. Snakes are the absolute worst. I just can't."

"Me too," Romy said. "Want to go inside and refill that cup?"

"Yes," Birdie responded. "With all my heart."

Romy encircled their arms as they made a beeline toward the house. Once inside, she let out the breath she'd been holding.

"Coffee is this way," Birdie led them to the kitchen and the coffee pot. Her stress levels were through the roof. She flexed and released her fingers a couple of times to work off some of the tension.

"What is it that you do for a living, Birdie?" Romy asked, pouring a cup for herself.

"I've been working odd jobs, saving up to start a small business," Birdie admitted.

"What kind of business?" Romy asked, her face brightening.

"I had this idea to make gourmet doughnuts," Birdie said. "But I don't know if it's a viable business or not."

"Sounds amazing," Romy said with genuine interest. She moved to the island and cradled the cup of coffee in her hands. "I'd love to hear more about it."

"It's just a pipe dream at this point. I highly doubt I'll ever get the money to make a real go of it now." She shrugged like it was no big deal but it hurt saying the words.

"Because of Meg's health?" Romy asked.

"Yes," Birdie admitted. It felt surprisingly good to talk about it. "I had money saved before, but she needed it for medical expenses. She's been so good to me ever since my mother died. I wanted to take care of her for a change."

"That's pretty amazing actually," Romy said as Birdie

refilled her cup. The caffeine was starting to kick in. Thankfully.

"It doesn't seem like much compared to all that she'd done for me," Birdie admitted.

"Setting your own dreams aside to care for someone you love seems like a lot to me," Romy said.

"When you put it like that, I suppose it really was a big deal." Birdie smiled. "But Meg would do anything for me in a heartbeat."

"She sounds lovely," Romy said.

"What about you?" Birdie turned the tables. "How long have you and Eric been together?"

"Funny story," Romy started as her cheeks turned three shades of pink. "We haven't known each other very long. Except that we have, if you know what I mean. I met him and knew there was something different about him straight out of the gate. I'm not sure I realized how special he was going to become in my life in a short period of time, but I got up to speed quickly."

"How did you know he was the one?" Birdie asked.

"It just became really obvious to me that I was never going to meet anyone else who lifted me up in the way he did. I didn't want to leave his side, but I chalked that up to attraction," Romy said.

"The Firebrand men do seem to have hit the genetic lotto," Birdie said with a laugh.

The front door opened, and Fallon and Eric walked in.

"Who hit what lotto?" Fallon asked.

Birdie and Romy exchanged glances before they both broke out into laughter. It had been a tense morning. A break was more than welcomed.

"No one is talking about nothing in here," Romy said before taking a sip of coffee and giving Birdie another look.

"I was just telling Romy about some plans I made once," Birdie said.

"And hopefully will resurrect soon," Romy added. She leaned over to Birdie and whispered, "I started a successful bakery from the ground up a few years ago and recently sold it. If you ever have any questions or I can help in any way, give me a shout."

"I might just take you up on that offer someday." Birdie located her cell and handed it to Romy. "Mind if I get your contact information?"

"Not at all," Romy said, taking the offering before plugging in her data.

"Thank you." Making a run at starting a business at this point seemed like a wild idea. If she decided to go for it, Romy would be the first person Birdie would call. Speaking of phone calls, she wanted to check on Meg. Birdie excused herself before heading out to the front porch. She immediately scanned the area for any other critters that might want to pay a visit.

Outside, it also dawned on her *a person* had placed the snake inside her vehicle. Would that same person be watching now? A shiver raced up her spine.

"ALL I KNEW yesterday is that you were coming home," Eric said. "How did you end up bringing Birdie here?"

"Long story," Fallon quipped. He wasn't ready to discuss his relationship with Birdie with anyone just yet. He couldn't. There wasn't a label on it yet.

"She showed up at the ranch?" Eric continued.

"I pulled her out of a ditch. Well, Bronc helped." Fallon realized his brother was trying to piece together why a complete stranger would end up an overnight guest at his place. "She swerved to miss a fawn and got herself into a tight spot. I was on my way home, and she looked like she needed a hand."

"She seems like a good person," Romy interjected. "I talked to her for a few minutes, and I have to say that I like her a lot."

Despite only having just met his sister-in-law, Fallon couldn't agree more with her assessment.

"What about the will?" Eric asked.

"I didn't tell her who I was on the road," Fallon admitted. "You know what comes with our last name. I didn't mind remaining anonymous a little while longer."

"Once you helped her out of the ditch without asking for anything in return, she realized she could trust you," Romy said.

Eric's eyebrow shot up but then he nodded his understanding. His wife would know how women thought better than the pair of them would.

"I'm pretty certain she planned to sleep in her car last night," Fallon admitted. "It was the reason for the invite to stay here. I couldn't very well stand by and let that happen."

"She mentioned her grandmother's illness," Romy said. "Her financial situation has drastically changed."

"Don't either of you take this the wrong way, but what makes you so certain both of them aren't gold diggers?" Eric asked as the door opened and Birdie stepped inside. A moment of shock darkened her features.

"I just came in to say goodbye," she said. "I'm, um, needed back home, so..."

"Hold on," Fallon said. "Don't leave without breakfast."

"Meg isn't picking up the phone. I should start back in case something's happened to her and she can't get to it." A look of terror passed behind her eyes as she made her way to the chair where she'd left her purse.

"How long is the drive?" Fallon asked.

"A few hours," she admitted, shouldering her bag.

"Wouldn't it be faster to call your sheriff and ask for a wellness check?" he asked. "A deputy might be able to get there in ten minutes."

She shifted her weight from foot to foot, and the chewed on the inside of her cheek. "I still need to head out."

"This might give you peace of mind while you make the drive," he continued, figuring he was making progress. If she'd allow it, he could hire someone to step in. He just didn't figure she would go for the idea and he hadn't come up with a good enough argument to make his case. He would, though, given enough time. "Besides, I can't send you away hungry."

Birdie looked to Romy and back. She must have received the confirmation she needed because she gave a small nod.

"How do I ask for the wellness check?" she asked as her cell phone buzzed in her hand. She jumped and gasped before checking the screen. "It's Meg."

The woman couldn't get back to the front porch fast enough.

"You're concerned the rattlesnake was just the beginning, aren't you?" Eric asked as he studied Fallon. Thankfully, Birdie was out of earshot.

He'd felt his brother's eyes on him. It had been a long time since they'd been in the same room. Despite growing up together and knowing each other for their entire early lives, they didn't know the men they'd grown into.

"I'd be lying if I said otherwise," Fallon admitted.

"Then, we need to come up with a plan," Eric stated. "You were stalling with the breakfast idea, am I right?"

"You are correct," Fallon said. His brother was keen. He'd give him that.

"What are you thinking next?" Eric asked.

"That I need to find a way to convince Birdie to let me help her and her grandmother," Fallon said. "The will has opened a can of worms and I'm afraid the snake is just the tip of the iceberg once news gets out."

"In that case, her grandmother could be in danger," Eric agreed.

"Have you thought about having Meg brought to the property to stay for a while?" Romy asked. She'd been quiet up to now, thinking.

"I'm not sure what her condition is or what doctors she needs to be close to, but the thought had crossed my mind," Fallon admitted.

"Those are good points. You could always go back with her," Romy said. "What could it hurt to have a little extra protection with her?"

"If she'd allow it," Fallon said.

"It never hurts to ask," Romy urged. His sister-in-law had a twinkle in her eye that told him she was up to something. Matchmaking?

If, and that was a very big *if*, Fallon was in the market for a girlfriend, he had no problems finding one on his own.

Birdie opened the door, and then came inside. Her face muscles were still bunched up and her breathing shallow.

"How is Meg?" Romy immediately asked.

"She's okay. Although, she has a bad habit of trying to make me believe she's fine when she's the opposite," Birdie said on a sigh.

"What do you think about the possibility of bringing her here?" Fallon asked.

"Oh, I'm not sure about that. I hadn't really thought

about it and I just don't know if that would be a good idea." Birdie seemed to be tripping over her words.

"Hear me out," Fallon said, locking gazes. It was probably a mistake considering the effect she had on him. Birdie was like a lightning striking on a sunny day without a cloud in sight. Her honesty was a breath of fresh air. "We can bring in the best doctors to treat her condition. We can set up a hospital-like atmosphere in this very room. Bring in specialists to make her more comfortable and get different points of view."

"I mean, that sounds amazing but..." She glanced around the room like she was searching for someone to reassure her that she was on the right track. "She already has her doctors in Austin and she's on a treatment plan."

"That last thing I want is for you to feel ganged up on," Romy hedged. "But more opinions couldn't hurt. The Firebrands could bring in the best in the country to take a look at Meg and see if there's anything else that could be done."

"It all sounds amazing and I'm grateful, so please don't take this the wrong way. I just can't accept this level of generosity. Meg wouldn't like feeling like a charity case," she said.

"She isn't," Fallon quickly clarified. "Meg was important to the Marshall or he wouldn't have wanted to leave her any money. Believe me when I say the man didn't exactly go around spreading cash to strangers."

Birdie nodded, but he could see that he wasn't making the progress he'd hoped for with her.

"There's something else, Birdie. Another reason I'm concerned about you leaving here and the relative safety of the ranch," he admitted.

She gasped, bringing her hand up to cover her mouth.

"You think the rattlesnake might just be the beginning," she said so low he almost couldn't hear her.

"I don't know what this is, but I'm not willing to risk your or Meg's safety to find out," he admitted.

Birdie was quiet for a long moment as she seemed to be running through all the possible dangers.

"The truth is that the rattlesnake might be a blip. You might leave here and be fine. Nothing else could happen," he continued while he had her attention. "But if you leave here and something *does* happen, I'm going to feel like a jerk for letting you walk out the door without giving this my best shot."

"But I was here when the rattlesnake was placed inside my car," she said. "An argument could be made that I might be safer out there."

"If someone can get to you here with all the security, think what might happen without it," Fallon said. "I haven't been home in a long time and I don't have the lay of the land here anymore. But my brothers do and I trust them to give us the right advice to keep you and Meg safe while all this gets sorted out."

"I have work," she countered. "Meg has bills that have to be paid."

"Believe me when I say money isn't a problem," he said.

"You have money," she countered. "We don't. There's a big difference."

"Not in my book," he argued. "I have more zeroes in my bank account than any one person would ever need. I'd like to use that money for good. I'd like to help you and Meg."

"Meg's medical bills are astronomical," Birdie countered. "It's the only reason I'm here in the first place. The will is supposed to be her way to cover the costs. But this is way more than I bargained for. Once I explain the situation to

Meg, she'll back off. She doesn't have the time or energy for a long court battle."

It suddenly dawned on him why she'd been ready to leave this morning. He'd taken it personally but it was all about being practical.

"What if you don't have to worry about that?" he asked.

Eric and Romy had gone quiet, huddling together at the island.

"That would be a miracle," she said. "But, honestly, I came here based on Meg's request. I'm really out of my comfort zone and I'm not used to taking charity from strangers."

"You could consider my help a down payment on Meg's inheritance," he said. "Would that make a difference?"

9

Fallon's offer was kind, and Birdie didn't see how she could refuse even though she'd always taken great pride in relying on herself. This wasn't about her. This was about Meg. Why was it so hard to say yes?

"There's a lot at stake with the new will," Fallon continued. "It could take years to sort out. I don't want to see someone you love suffer because my family can't get along."

"How would this work exactly?" she asked.

"In a perfect world, I'd like to bring Meg here to the ranch," he said.

Birdie was already shaking her head before he finished his sentence. "I highly doubt she would leave her home. She loves waking up surrounded by her art. Being able to work in her studio is half of what is keeping her fighting. Not to mention the fact her doctors are nearby."

"Experts can always be flown in no matter where she is," he agreed. "She wouldn't have to be here for that."

Birdie realized that they were in a whole different stratosphere when it came to having money. To be honest, it was all a little more than overwhelming, both the situation itself and Fallon's kindness. A mix of emotions threatened to bring tears to her eyes.

"I could come home with you," he offered.

"Why would you do that?" she asked, wishing she could take back the words as soon as they left her mouth. His generosity caught her off guard and his presence caused her world to tilt on its axis.

"Because I can. Because you need the help. Because the ranch can spare me a little while longer until I'm certain you and your grandmother are safe and have everything you need," he stated without hesitation.

She absolutely believed him. And yet, there was something he wasn't saying. What was it? Did he feel responsible for them somehow? Or was it something else? Something more personal? The reason he hadn't wanted to come to his home alone last night?

And then it dawned on her. Was he looking for a way to be useful after leaving the only life he'd known for more than a decade?

Birdie took in a slow breath, realizing she would do anything in her power to help Meg. Accepting Fallon's help on her grandmother's behalf didn't seem like such a chore when she thought about it like that. Plus, it seemed like she would be doing Fallon a favor, giving him time to get his bearings before diving into the family business.

"I'm sure Meg will appreciate whatever you're willing to do for her," Birdie conceded. "As do I."

Fallon looked to his brother. "You guys can spare me for a few days, right?"

"We'll do more than that. You can count on us to help in any capacity," Eric stated. Romy was already nodding. "Tell us what you need and we'll move mountains to get it."

Emotion welled up inside Birdie at the show of support.

The whole concept of having other people she could rely on was completely foreign to her, and would take time to adjust to, but was also a welcome change.

"I don't know what to say," she said. "But I'll start with thank you."

"We should get on the road soon," Fallon stated.

"We're a phone call or text away," Eric said before taking his wife's hand in his. The small smile shared between them stirred Birdie's heart.

She had been comfortable with Ethan. She cared deeply for him. She believed she loved him, and she did in a way. The tenderness happening between Eric and Romy wasn't something Birdie had experienced with Ethan or any of her exes for that matter. But then, she hadn't expected to feel that way about a boyfriend either. Had she been settling?

Her attraction to Fallon was in a stratosphere all by itself. Electricity hummed anytime he was in the same room and her stomach free fell every time their gazes touched. Don't even get her started on her body's reaction to the man. She became all tingles and warmth every time she looked at him.

Fallon Firebrand was easy on the eyes. Hard on the heart?

There was something about leaving the Firebrand Ranch that made Birdie surprisingly melancholy. She wanted, no needed to get back to Meg. No question there. And yet, leaving this place hit her square in the chest.

FALLON FOLLOWED Birdie in his truck, using the drive to Meg's house to make arrangements. There would be round-the-clock care provided from here on out. A discreet security van would be parked out front in her cul-de-sac driveway in case of emergency. The pair of guards inside would monitor the area via cameras.

Other than that, he'd arranged a meal service and help with chores. He had a feeling Birdie was used to doing everything alone, on top of working two jobs. All he could hope was that she would be willing to accept the services. He'd arranged for a liver cancer specialist to visit and provide an analysis to see if everything possible was being done for her care and comfort.

By the time they pulled up to the bungalow, the van was already in place. Birdie parked and immediately started toward the vehicle. Fallon jumped out of the driver's seat of his truck.

"Whoa there," he said to Birdie as she marched past him. "I hired those guys to keep an eye on things."

Birdie stopped in her tracks. She spun around. Her mouth opened and then snapped shut a couple of times like she was at a loss for words.

"I just thought you'd have more peace of mind if we had extra eyes on the place," he said, hoping he hadn't gone too far.

Her pulse pounded at the base of her throat, stirring a wave of thoughts he didn't need to be thinking right now.

"Thank you," she finally said with some effort. "I didn't realize...and my mind went to a dark place."

"It's understandable after what you've been through," he reassured. The shock of having a poisonous snake placed in her vehicle probably hadn't worn off. "But that's exactly why I thought it would be a good idea."

"It is," she quickly added. "It's just going to take me a minute to get used to this."

He gave a quick rundown of the other services he'd scheduled. Those big eyes grew wider.

"I don't know how I'll ever repay you for all this," she said.

"You won't have to," he said. "It seems like it's what the Marshall would have wanted."

"I hope you don't take this the wrong way, but how would you know if the two of you weren't close?" she asked.

"No. Not at all. In fact, I didn't know him well at all. I saw his bad side, though," he admitted. "Still, I regret to this day that I never got the chance to take the man out for a beer and clear the air between us. Now that he's gone, I'll never get the opportunity."

"Oh," she said. His explanation seemed to resonate. "That makes a whole lot of sense actually."

"If Meg was important to him, maybe she can shed some light on a better side to the man than any of us back home ever saw," he continued.

"It won't be weird to hear about him from his mistress?" She cocked an eyebrow.

"When you put it like that...yes," he said with a chuckle. Hearing the words spoke out loud definitely put the situation in a different light.

"Sorry," she said. "That sounded harsh."

"It was honest," he admitted. "I'm looking at this whole situation as a chance to get to know a different side to the Marshall."

"There had to be something good about him or Meg never would have spent time with him," Birdie hedged.

"I'd like to know what she saw," he said.

"Okay, then. Follow me." With that, Birdie walked past him and to her vehicle to retrieve her things.

His duffel was still packed, so he'd been ready to go once

the decision to leave had been made. He motioned toward her bag. "Can I help you with that?"

"I got it," she said. Given how difficult it was for her let him do something as simple as carry a bag for her, he realized how far out of her comfort zone she must be in accepting the amount of help he would be providing in the coming days and weeks. His respect and admiration for her grew even more. It was easy to see how much she loved Meg. He had another idea he wanted to pitch to Birdie but didn't want to short circuit her all in one day. At present, he didn't know how close to the line he was stepping.

Birdie stopped on the small concrete porch barely large enough for two people. She spun around and the two were chest to face. Fallon would take a step back if it didn't mean falling. An electrical current so strong it robbed Fallon's ability to speak coursed through him. His throat dried up on him, and his pulse skyrocketed. She was beautiful in every sense of the word. Outwardly, she was as close to perfect as one could be with those wide eyes, full lips. He tightened his grip on his duffel to stop from reaching a hand to touch her creamy skin.

"I, uh, wanted to warn you that I have no idea what shape the place is in since I left yesterday," Birdie's breathy voice dipped a couple of octaves. It sounded sexy as all get out and he had to remind himself to breathe through the fist in his chest.

"We'll deal with it," he said, hearing the huskiness in his own tone. "You're not alone anymore, Birdie."

An emotion passed behind her eyes that he couldn't quite pinpoint. Shock mixed with relief? Her autumn-colored eyes glittered with something that looked a lot like need, with did little to quell the attraction taking on a life of its own inside him.

"Okay." Birdie cleared her throat and spun back around. He had no idea if she was ready to accept the change in circumstances but she seemed at least like she wouldn't fight it. Good, because there was one more gift he wanted to be able to give her and Meg. Time.

Again, he didn't think she was quite ready to hear his proposal.

Birdie opened the door, and he followed her inside. The place could best be described as cozy. Art lined the walls, a bookshelf, and almost every visible space. Despite the sheer amount in such a small area, there was a good flow to the room and décor. The place didn't look cluttered as it would if all this was in Fallon's house. He had no eye for decorating. The work was unmistakable because it mirrored the Marshall's prize possession, the palomino at the front entry.

A frail woman sitting in a recliner with a folding tray table beside her and an afghan draped over her perked up.

"Birdie," the woman he assumed was Meg said, clapping her hands together. "You're all grown up."

"I'm here." Birdie dropped her bag, and scurried over to Meg's side. "And I brought a friend who will be staying with us for a few days. I hope that's okay."

"Your mother will be beside herself worried," Meg said.

As far as Fallon knew, Birdie's mother had passed away. Did Meg have dementia on top of her diagnosis? Could be medications. There were a dozen pill bottles on the little table.

"Did Ms. Winzel stop by this morning?" Birdie asked, but Meg had already lost interest. The woman's gaze landed on Fallon, she gasped and clasped her hands together next to her cheek.

"Marshall? Is that you?" Meg asked in a voice filled with hope.

The picture window to his back must have cast a shadow on his face. Fallon had been called many things in his life, but Marshall had never been one of them.

"No, ma'am. I'm his grandson." Fallon stepped closer, hoping she could get a better look at his face.

"You look so much like him," Meg said, and she seemed to be trying hard to hide her disappointment. "Is he here?"

She took great effort in trying to see around Fallon.

"No, ma'am," Fallon said. "It's just Birdie and me."

"Birdie," Meg exclaimed. "Your mother will be worried sick about you if you don't get home soon."

"I'm fine, Meg. I promise." Birdie's forehead creased with concern. She looked caught off guard by Meg's repetition. His mind snapped back to the medications. He made a mental note to check with the pharmacist later for possible drug interactions. Based on his sister-in-law Prudence's memory loss experience due to a new drug Eric had mentioned in his update, Fallon figured it was better to be safe than sorry.

The cozy living room was open to a dining area. Off to the left seemed like a kitchen area. It wasn't visible to the living room. A hallway off the living room most likely led to bedrooms and a bathroom. The living area housed a pair of matching recliners with a table in between large enough to hold a lamp and not a whole lot else. Across from the recliners, a velvet bench ran just shy of the length of the bookshelves behind it.

"Meg is an artist," Birdie said. There was so much pride in her voice.

"Did you make all this?" He glanced around the room.

Meg smiled. She was probably a good ten pounds underweight for her frame. Her green eyes sparkled when she talked. "I did. It's my life's work."

"I hope you're not finished yet," he encouraged. "I'd like to see what else your mind creates."

"Sitting up for long periods is a little difficult right now," she admitted on a sigh. Her long gray hair was neatly piled on top of her head.

"How long has that been going on?" he asked.

"Since I got sick, I suppose," she said with a shrug, then motioned toward the bench. "Where are my manners? Please. Have a seat."

Fallon thanked her and did as she requested.

"Would you like something to drink?" Meg asked, reaching for the button that would bring the recliner upright.

"Stay here and talk," Birdie said. "I can get Fallon something to drink. "

"Fallon is a lovely name," Meg said after agreeing to ease back down in her chair. She patted down a few errant strands of hair.

"Thank you," he said.

"What can I get you for you?" Birdie asked. "There was iced tea, lemonade, and Coke last time I checked."

"Water is fine," he said.

"That's easy enough," she quipped. The tension lines on Birdie's face relaxed now that she saw Meg was doing fine. Good.

Birdie disappeared around the corner where he'd guessed the kitchen was located.

Meg leaned forward like she was about to spill a secret. "Her mother is going to be worried sick if she doesn't go home soon."

Fallon nodded and smiled. Checking her medication jumped up the priority scale.

"It's been a busy day," Meg said on a sigh. "I've had so many visitors."

"You don't usually have many?" he asked, figuring her mind couldn't exactly be counted on at this point.

"My neighbor checks on me every morning," she said.

"Ms. Winzel?" he asked.

"Why, yes. How did you know?" Meg seemed genuinely surprised. "Are you from around here?"

"No, ma'am," he said as Birdie brought over a glass of water. She set one on Meg's table as well before retreating to the kitchen. She came back with a glass of what looked like iced tea for herself. "Who else stopped by to see you today?"

"Ms. Winzel's son William," she exclaimed.

Birdie's eyebrow shot up.

"What did he look like?" she asked, giving a quick look at Fallon.

"He wasn't tall like him." She motioned toward Fallon. Then, lowered her voice when she said, "And he didn't have the physique." She wiggled her eyebrows and they laughed.

"What color was his hair?" Birdie asked, and he could tell she was drawing a blank on who this person might be. Alarm bells sounded.

"Sandy-blond and he had the bluest blue eyes I've ever seen. He looked like one of those…" she snapped her fingers. "Joggers you might see at the park. You know, tall and thin."

Birdie's gaze unfocused like she was looking inside herself trying to come up with a name. She gave a small shake. "Was this person wearing scrubs?"

"Nope. He had on slacks, a collared shirt, and a black hat," she supplied.

More warning bells sounded. No real cowboy or rancher wore a black hat in the heat of summer in Texas. This guy was playing a role, trying to blend in. He either wasn't from around here or didn't have anything else to cover his face. Fallon locked eyes with Birdie. It was possible a black hat was all this person had on hand to block his face from others. Since neighbors were spread out in this area, wearing a hat would make it that much more difficult to get identifying information like hair color and facial features.

Fallon made eyes at Birdie, and she seemed to catch on right away.

"Did William stay long?" Birdie asked.

"No. Not very." Meg got a sheepish look on her face. "I'm afraid I wasn't very good company. I closed my eyes for a few seconds, and then he was gone."

10

Birdie didn't want to create a panic, but this news was unsettling to say the least. No one was scheduled to drop by other than Ms. Winzel. Fallon didn't seem to have sent anyone, either. The most troubling part was the fact Meg's memory couldn't be trusted. The way she kept repeating herself was worrying. It wasn't something she normally did.

"Did William say why he stopped by?" Meg asked, taking a seat on the other recliner. She perched on the edge, and set her tea down next to the lamp.

"Nope. He sure didn't. I suspect he was making sure I was okay," Meg said with a shrug.

Since this seemed like a dead end, Birdie decided to shift gears. "When was the last time you ate something?"

"Don't worry about me," Meg said. "Ask our guest if he's hungry."

"We're good," Birdie said. "Fallon is going to be staying with us for a couple of days, if that's okay."

"We haven't had a house guest in a long time," she said. "Too long, if you ask me."

"It's settled then," Birdie continued. "Fallon will keep you company while I work tomorrow."

"Oh?" Meg perked up again. "Sounds like I have a date."

"Yes, ma'am," Fallon said.

Meg squinted at him. "I've missed you."

Did she think he was Marshall again? Birdie's concern levels shot through the roof.

"On second thought, I am a little hungry," Fallon said. "How about I give you a hand in the kitchen?"

"Okay," Birdie drew out the word, not sure where he was going with this.

Meg clapped her hands together.

"I'll just take a teensy nap, so I'll be fresh and ready to stay up late and talk," Meg said. She didn't seem to realize it was barely noon.

Birdie grabbed her iced tea and headed for the kitchen. She could hear Fallon's footsteps behind her if not sense his presence. Her body seemed to know when he was near. His spicy male scent, all clean and warm, filled her senses in the tight space with every intake of air.

She turned around and planted her hands on the bull-nose edge of the granite countertop. "Do you have any idea why this 'William' would stop by?"

"Not a clue," Fallon admitted. With him standing this close, her nerves settled a notch below panic. There was something calming about being in a room with this man.

"I have to say it." She lowered her voice. "Meg could be hallucinating."

"Does she normally repeat herself?" he asked.

"Not like this," she stated.

"My first thought is medicine interaction. Has she gotten any new prescriptions recently?" he continued.

"No. But now I'm wondering if Ms. Winzel gave Meg the

wrong dose of her medications this morning," Birdie stated, shaking her head and looking at a loss. "She's so careful, though. I can't imagine it,"

"Meg might have forgotten that she already took her pills," he added. "She could have repeated a dose."

"Which is why she can't be left alone." A stab of guilt wracked Birdie. "I shouldn't have listened to her and gone to the ranch."

Fallon's face twisted.

Had she offended him? "I didn't mean…"

He waved her off.

"I, for one, am glad you came to Lone Star Pass," he said. "If I'm honest with myself, being home was a lot more than I bargained for. I thought I was ready but didn't realize what I was coming back to."

"It's paradise at the ranch," she quickly said.

"The place itself is as I remember. But everyone changed. It's been a long time since I was home and I underestimated how I would react to all the differences," he admitted.

"Nothing stands still," she agreed.

"Which is why I hope you'll hear me out with what I have to say next." He locked gazes with her, causing her heart to hammer the inside of her ribcage.

"I'm listening." She dropped her gaze to the tile flooring.

"Don't go back to work," he said. Before she could argue, he put up his hands in the surrender position. "Hear me out before you decide."

Birdie took in a long, slow breath before nodding.

"Let me give you the gift of time with Meg," he said. "It would be the best way I can think of to honor the Marshall's memory."

"You're already doing so much," she said. "And how do

you know your grandfather would have wanted you to do any of this?"

"Looking around, it's become clear to me how much she meant to him. The palomino horse in the entryway was the closest to his heart," he said. "And he didn't care much about owning anything."

Birdie compressed her lips. Under normal circumstances, there was no way she would even consider his request. Complicated didn't begin to describe this situation. The thought of being home with Meg to care for the woman who had been Birdie's rock was almost more than she could process. Taking charity from someone in order to do it was a whole different ballgame.

"I'm not doing nearly enough," he said. "If the Marshall wanted to acknowledge Meg in his will at one time not all that long ago, she must have been very special to him."

Birdie nodded but held her tongue.

"I feel like I can get to know my grandfather a little better by being with Meg and getting to know the kind of person he cared about," he continued. "Believe me, he never once gave any of us the impression he cared about anyone or anything other than Texas and his ranch. I don't have the best memories of him. We didn't go fishing together. He didn't teach me how to ride a bike. We had no real connection outside of both loving the ranch business. Meg is a window to another side of him that I've never seen." He paused for a beat. "I've lost the opportunity to take the man out for a beer, but I can do this. I can make Meg's money troubles disappear and I can give you time to be with her. What kind of jerk would I be if I just kept all that money in a building when it can be out here doing some good in the world?"

Fallon made for a convincing argument. She had to give

him that much. The pain in his voice—pain that he did try to cover—nearly ripped her heart out of her chest.

How could she deny him the opportunity to help someone who had been important to his grandfather? How could she say no to a man who was as broken and conflicted as she? How could she stop him from doing something he believed in?

"I'll let my bosses know that I won't be coming back to work for a while," she said.

"Bosses?" he asked, a dark brow shot up.

"I've been working two jobs to support us," she admitted, and then exhaled. Really exhaled. It had been so long since she felt like she could really breathe.

Fallon brought his hands up to cup her face. His touch was surprisingly tender. He feathered a kiss on her lips that caused her stomach to free fall. "You are a remarkable person, Birdie. Thank you for letting me step up and do the right thing by Meg."

A rogue tear fell down her cheek. He thumbed it away. She attempted to duck her head, so she could hide her face but he stopped her.

"You're beautiful," he said, and his voice was gravelly. That voice threatened to break the walls she'd constructed after Ethan.

Birdie couldn't allow them to come down. Not with a man who could shatter her.

Fallon didn't want to cross a point of no return with Birdie, so he dropped his hands to his sides. He'd noticed she had a habit of looking away when emotions started getting the best of her. With effort, he resisted the temptation to touch that beautiful face again.

"I'm here to help in any way I can," he stated, guiding the conversation back on course after crossing a line he probably should leave untouched. The kiss had lasted only a second or two and his lips had barely touched hers, and yet his soul stirred. Since that was about as smart as sticking his hand in a campfire and holding it there, he'd backed off.

"Much appreciated," she said, and her voice was husky.

He couldn't deny it felt good to have a sense of purpose. The military life had been straightforward, easy compared to the civilian world. There, he had marching orders. Not here. The problem was that Fallon had been in the service so long he'd forgotten where it ended and he began.

"I have home healthcare aids scheduled to come at six and eleven a.m., then at three and seven p.m. for the time being. I left nights open but figured this would give you enough breaks throughout the day to be able to work on getting the finances in order," he said.

"Wow, that all sounds amazing," she said, clearing her throat. "You have no idea how much time it takes to straighten out medical billing."

"I can only imagine," he stated. "I'd like to go ahead and check with a pharmacist about possible drug interactions. Douglas Grainger used to be our go-to pharmacist growing up. With nine boys, I'm pretty certain Mom had him and our pediatrician on speed dial."

Birdie smiled. More of those tension lines relaxed, and he swelled with pride thinking he had something to do with the change. She was clearly someone who worked hard, and her heart was bigger than the Texas sky. Good people like her deserved a break in life.

"It was just me and my mom growing up," she said. Her

cheeks tinted a shade of pink with the admission. "She worked most of the time, which was fine. I took care of myself mostly."

He was beginning to understand how deep her independence ran. Strong women were sexy, but he saw nothing wrong with moments of weakness, either. Life was a pendulum where both great happiness and great sadness had their places.

Not that he could talk. He'd been stuffing down his feelings about his homecoming since returning to the ranch. Talking to Birdie was easy, though. She made him want to speak up when he would normally shut down.

Birdie motioned toward the table and chairs next to the kitchen area. "I can keep an eye on Meg better from there."

He nodded, and then took a seat.

"Mom was great, and she did the best she could with what she had to work with," Birdie continued after claiming a spot that allowed her a visual connection to Meg. "Mom dated around a little when she had time."

"And your father?" He'd noticed she hadn't mentioned him, and hoped he wasn't hitting a sore spot.

"There isn't much to tell there. I never met him," she said like it was no big deal. "Mom only brought home the ones she was serious with, but no one ever stuck around for too long."

"Have you ever been curious about him? Your father?" he continued, treading lightly.

"When I was about fifteen, I went through an identity crisis," she said with a wistful smile. "I did a little bit of digging around, and even located him on social media. He was holding a baby in his arms, and he had this proud look on his face. He had a new family. I realized right then that he'd moved on and so should I. There was no use pining for someone who wouldn't love me back. You know?"

He nodded. He knew better than he wanted to admit. His father might have lived under the same roof but he'd never been the type to kiss his kids goodnight or offer an *I love you.*

"To be honest, I spent a few months licking my wounds before I got to the place where I could let it go," she said before nodding toward Meg. "That one there has always been my rock through all my ups and downs. And piercings." Again, her cheeks turned a few shades of pink before she said, "I'm talking too much."

"It's all good," he reassured. "I've been surrounded by a whole lot of smelly soldiers for too many years who do little more than crack jokes about each other's bathroom habits. Plus, it's a nice change of pace to talk about something besides how many seconds someone can hold a burp."

Her face broke into a wide smile. More of that tension seemed to roll off.

"It's a sad truth. Throw too many guys together and the jokes go south real quick," he said. "Besides, I want to know more about you." Then he added, "It helps me get to know Meg better."

Fallon had no idea why he'd felt the need to add the last part, except that things were perhaps getting too personal, too fast with Birdie. He wasn't ready to think about just how much he was enjoying getting to know her, so part of him needed to pull back.

The flash of hurt in Birdie's eyes was a gut punch. The wall that came up between them showed him just how much of a fool he'd been.

Birdie snapped her fingers as an idea lit up her eyes. "What if William came here looking for something?"

"Something like a will?" he asked.

"Exactly," she said. "It's possible Meg mentioned the will to someone. Although, I can't imagine Ms. Winzel would tell anyone."

"Small towns and gossip go together like cheese on nachos," he said. "Where do people hang out and talk?"

"The diner for one," she said. "The post office can be a big gathering spot on Mondays and Fridays."

"I'm sure your neighbor is well-meaning, but if she's like most, she probably enjoys having something to talk about," he said.

"She's a sweetheart, but that definitely describes her to a T," Birdie said.

"Word might have gotten around about the will," he reasoned. It was probably a long shot but it was all they had to go on for now.

"I guess so." Birdie seemed to be thinking along the same lines.

Hold on a minute. Meg's bad memory timed with the visitor gave Fallon an idea. He quietly walked over to the medicine table. Birdie followed. There was a pill container with each dose for the day in a separate compartment. He picked up the plastic container, and then brought it back to the table.

He opened up a couple of the 'days' of the week, and immediately took note of the difference in tomorrow's dose.

"Does Meg normally take a different set of pills on—"

Birdie gasped. Her hand came up to cover her mouth.

"The blue pill doesn't belong in here," she said. "I've never seen it before."

"This could explain Meg's repetition earlier," he stated.

"And the fact she's already asleep," Birdie added.

Fallon couldn't get to Meg fast enough. He checked her pulse. "It's weak and her breathing is shallow."

"I'll call 911," Birdie said. Her phone was out before he could say another word.

This William character showing up on a day a random pill ended up in Meg's pill box couldn't be a coincidence. Someone was trying to get rid of her. And Fallon didn't want to consider the fact the *someone* could share the last name Firebrand.

11

"Wake up, Meg." Birdie gently shook her grandmother's shoulders.

Meg's eyes blinked open, but they almost immediately closed again.

"Stay with me," Birdie pleaded, wiping a few rogue tears from her cheeks. "Can you wake up?"

Meg mumbled something unintelligible.

The next twenty minutes were the longest of Birdie's life. A pair of EMTs arrived, Al and Hank. The two men managed to lift Meg onto a gurney without disturbing her. Al broke open a packet of something, and then placed it underneath Meg's nose. Her face wrinkled as she blinked her eyes open again.

"Ma'am, stay with us," Al said. His partner, Hank, helped lift the handrails.

"She might have taken something we can't identify," Birdie stated again, in case dispatch hadn't passed along the message.

"Do you have the substance?" Hank asked.

"Yes, there's a pill in here that shouldn't be," Birdie said as she held up the pillbox.

"Bring that with you to the hospital, okay?" Hank said. "The doctor will want to take a look. In the meantime, Miss Meg's condition is stabilized for now. We're going to take her to county."

"We'll meet you there," Birdie said. She glanced at Fallon who had grabbed her handbag and had keys in hand.

Fallon linked their fingers after she locked the door behind them. They darted toward his truck, which was parked behind Blue Jay. He signaled to the security van that was parked in the cul-de-sac to keep eyes on the home. She only wished they'd gotten there sooner.

Birdie's entire world felt like it was crashing down around her. Meg had been sick recently. Very sick. And yet, Birdie hadn't been able to process the fact her grandmother wouldn't be around much longer. She still couldn't accept the reality of the situation. The thought of losing her today gutted Birdie.

Rather than try to hold in the torrent of emotion, she let the floodgates open. A sob racked her. Then, another. And another. Finally no longer stuffing her emotions down. Tears fell as her body released all the pent-up sadness she'd been feeling.

Fallon pulled into a parking spot at the hospital, took off his seatbelt, and then suddenly she was in his arms. He held her against his chest and she was comforted by the rhythm of his beating heart. In that moment, time seemed to warp, and they got caught in the wave.

Birdie had no idea how long they were there. It felt like an eternity and no time at all. He whispered a whole lot of reassurances in her ear, promises they both knew he couldn't guarantee.

When her sobs finally subsided, he said, "You tell me

when you're ready to go inside. There's no rush. Meg is likely still with the doctor. Going in now or sitting here a few more minutes won't make a difference."

His words comforted her, and she wanted to hold onto his strength just a little while longer. She needed to take a minute to breathe, to really breathe before heading inside to the waiting room.

After the snake in her vehicle this morning and now the mystery medicine, it was clear someone was trying to erase Birdie and her grandmother. It was safe to say news of the will must be out. But how?

"Someone is working fast," Birdie finally said, pulling back from Fallon.

"The person must be counting on the element of surprise." He linked their fingers, and the connection calmed Birdie's rattled nerves. "In fact, I need to update Lawler and alert my family."

Birdie nodded.

Fallon let go of her hand long enough to fire off several texts. "The sheriff will want to cooperate with local law enforcement."

"Sharing information is good," she said.

"I'd like to swing by and speak to your neighbors," he added. "Find out if they saw anyone earlier today, a vehicle, or have any information about the visit from this 'William' person."

"I'll call Ms. Winzel right now," Birdie said, retrieving her cell from her handbag. "Meg's thoughts are clearly confused, so…"

A scary thought struck. Could that 'someone' have followed them to the hospital?

"Should we go inside? Is Meg safe?" she asked.

"This is a very public place with lots of witnesses,"

Fallon reassured. "If there's an overnight stay, we definitely want to put security at her door but while she's being treated, she should be fine."

The reality of a person walking into Meg's home with the intention of doing harm was a gut punch. If Birdie had known any of this was a possibility, she never would have gone to the Firebrand Ranch in the first place. Then again, hindsight was always 20/20 and she had no way of knowing beforehand.

Birdie shot off a text to Ms. Winzel, asking if she knew anyone by the name of William. "I may not hear back for a while. Ms. Winzel frequently leaves her phone in a different room and forgets it's there. I don't know how many times she's made the comment she should learn to keep it in her pocket."

"It would be nice if someone could give us a trail to follow," he said.

"Any ideas on who might do something like this?" Birdie asked. The rattlesnake attack had happened at the ranch and within hours of her producing the will.

"Definitely not Adam or Prudence." He shook his head. "They were the first to find out."

His gaze widened and then he thumped his pad of his thumb on the steering wheel. "I need to call my brother."

Birdie gripped her cell, willing her body to stop trembling at the thought someone wanted her and Meg dead.

"Adam, I'm sitting in the parking lot of a hospital. Mind if I put you on speaker?" Fallon asked. His brother must have agreed because Fallon moved the cell away from his ear and tapped the screen. "Birdie is here."

"What's going on? Are you guys okay?" Adam's voice was laced with concern. Again, Birdie noted how nice it was to have such a large, tight-knit family.

"Yes," Fallon said. "We're fine but someone slipped a pill in Birdie's grandmother's pillbox. We're about to go inside but it just dawned on me that only two people knew about the will last night."

"That would be me and my wife," he stated.

"Unless it isn't," Fallon said. "Are you in the main house?"

"Yes," Adam confirmed.

"Can you go outside so we can talk?" Fallon asked.

"Okay-y-y," Adam drew out the word. The sound of a door opening and closing came through the line. And then it seemed to dawn on Adam. He lowered his voice to Sunday service quiet when he said, "Hold on a minute. You aren't saying what I think you are...are you?"

"You offered to let me sleep at the main house. People come and go. It's a big place and I have a question," Fallon stated.

"What if it's bugged?" Adam caught on immediately.

"You talked about what was in the will," Birdie chimed in. "We had a conversation about it."

Adam let out a string of curses.

"It's the only thing that makes sense," Fallon said.

"I can't begin to count how many people have been in the house over the past few days, let alone weeks," Adam stated.

"If someone was trying to get to the Marshall, they could have been visiting him when he was alive. I'm sure Lawler will want a list of known names," Fallon said.

"He contacted me a couple of minutes ago," Adam said. "He'll be conducting interviews of everyone on property. I told him he could use the kitchen, but now it would probably be better if he sets up the interviews somewhere else."

"I'm certain he'll want to sweep the house for any traces of bugs," Fallon said.

"True," Adam agreed. "I was just thinking the same thing."

"Would you mind keeping me posted?" Fallon asked.

"Will do," came the quick response. The pair exchanged goodbyes before ending the call.

The list of suspects seemed to grow exponentially with the update. Birdie should have checked Meg's house to see if anything was out of place in the bedroom where she stored valuables and papers. First things first, Birdie needed to get inside the hospital and get an update on her grandmother.

"YOUR GRANDMOTHER IS GOING to be fine."

Fallon figured those words from the doctor had to be the best Birdie had heard all day. She'd been pacing up and down the hallway for the last thirty minutes. Despite him knowing she had to be hungry, she'd refused to eat until word came about Meg.

"I'm Dr. Devinsky." The older gentleman wore scrubs and a lab coat that bore his name. He had a stethoscope draped around his neck, and a kind smile. He shook Birdie's then Fallon's hand.

"Thank you so much," Birdie said as she finally seemed to exhale.

"The pill contains a heavy dose of acetaminophen," Dr. Devinsky explained.

"Isn't that sold over-the-counter for headaches?" Birdie asked.

"Yes, and too much, which is surprisingly easy to overdo, is lethal," he said.

"So a few of these pills and we might not have gotten to her in time?" she asked.

"That's right. There's a point of no return with acetaminophen," he continued. "Fortunately, that's not where we are with your grandmother. We're giving her IV fluids and keeping her a few hours for observation. I expect she can go home afterward, where she'll rest more comfortably."

"I can't begin to thank you enough," Birdie said to the doctor. "Would it be possible for us to stay in the room with her in the meantime?" Fallon asked, not wanting to let Meg out of sight while she remained hospitalized. He didn't believe 'William' would come to such a crowded place, but Fallon didn't plan to take any chances either. There was no use bringing security here if Meg was truly going to be released in a few hours. His detail was best left at Meg's place where they could keep watch on the home.

"The nurse will lead you to her," the doctor said before turning to wave someone over.

A woman wearing scrubs walked over and introduced herself as Patsy. "I can show you to your grandmother's room now."

Birdie nodded and thanked the nurse, immediately following Patsy. Fallon followed suit, intentionally hanging back a few steps in order to check out anyone who seemed too interested in Birdie. All his protective instincts flared, and his military training kicked in.

He casually pulled his cell phone out and texted the security detail about the home breach. He gave over the few details they had about this 'William' character and explained what to watch for. Then, he updated his team about the pill situation as well as when he expected to return home from the hospital.

The response came almost immediately, along with an

update there had been no further activity on the cul-de-sac thus far.

Figuring his bases were covered, Fallon stopped at Meg's door so Birdie could have some privacy with her grandmother. He crossed his arms over his chest and stood in an athletic stance. This took him back to not-so-long ago while he was standing watch over a diplomatic family that was being moved out when the situation became hostile. That had been his job, and he'd been good at it. Fallon took pride in the number of successful extractions he'd contributed to.

Protecting Birdie was personal. It wasn't lost on him that he was in the civilian world now, and on his own. The rules were different here. Being home at the ranch, for instance, had been a stark reminder of how much he'd changed. Which also reminded him that his father had most likely been released from the hospital this morning. He owed his mother a call.

Fallon pulled her up in his contacts. His thumb hovered over the name as he stood there for a long moment, trying to figure out exactly what he was going to say. He figured he'd start with hello and see where the conversation went from there.

"Fallon?" His mom answered on the first ring.

"The one and only. How are you?" he asked for lack of something better. How did he explain his absence to the woman who gave birth to him and then cared for him his entire youth?

"Are you okay?" she asked.

"Yes, ma'am." He snapped into formal mode.

"It's so good to hear your voice. I'm so happy you called," she said, and he could hear the shock in her voice. "Your father is about to be released from the hospital so I can't talk long."

"That's good to hear," he said, then added, "the part about Dad being released."

Could this conversation be any lamer?

"Mom, I love you," he said, figuring he might not get that in if she had to in a hurry.

"I love you, too, son," she said with all the warmth and kindness in her voice he remembered. It would have been so easy for him to stay at the ranch where life would have just unfolded for him. But then who would he truly be?

"Where are you?" she asked.

"Texas," he said. "But I'm coming home soon."

There was a long, quiet pause. It was surprisingly comforting.

"For a visit?" she asked.

"For good," he reassured.

"Have you decided where you will live?" she continued.

"At my home on the ranch," he informed.

"We have much to celebrate," she said. "Many of your brothers are married and we haven't had a party for them. Your father is going to be fine. You've come home. It's the perfect reason for us all to celebrate and maybe start bringing in the pieces of this fractured family."

There was so much pride and happiness in her voice. So much hope. This was the Lucia Firebrand that Fallon remembered and loved. His father was more of a mystery, and it was time to unravel. After losing the Marshall while things were unsettled between them, Fallon made a promise to himself not to let that happen with his father. Like it or not, Brodie Firebrand was going to get to know his son. Having a beer together might be a long ways off, depending on his dad's recovery, but they could drink water for all he cared. Fallon had no intention of waiting. Time, he'd learned, was too precious.

Unfamiliar voices came through the line.

"Do you need to go?" he asked his mother.

"Yes, but that doesn't mean I want to," she admitted.

"I'm coming home," he reassured. "We'll see each other soon."

"Promise?" she asked as the voices got louder.

"You can't get rid of me that easily," he teased. "Go take care of your husband."

"Not without saying it one more time. I love you, Fallon. My sweet, independent boy," she said, and he could swear he heard her smiling.

He wasn't so sure about the 'sweet' part, but the independence he had down pat. The military had helped him realize the importance of working with others. Something he wasn't so sure he'd been good at growing up.

"Love you, Mom," he said one more time.

"See you soon." The hopeful sound of her voice, along with pure excitement mixed with a little bit of disbelief, warmed his heart. He didn't expect nearly the same warm reception from his father. *Fine,* he thought. The man wasn't going to get a choice anyway.

After hanging up, the weight that had been a heavy blanket wrapped around Fallon's shoulders for most of his life lifted just a little bit. He still hadn't forgiven his father for his indiscretions or lies, but the time had come to clear the air. One way or another, Fallon was going to figure out a way to do it while his father was still alive.

"Hey," Birdie said, cutting into his thoughts. A beam of light penetrated the heavy blanket, scoring a direct hit in the center of his chest. His warning systems engaged because this woman could do serious damage to his heart.

12

"How's Meg?"

The fact Fallon asked about Birdie's grandmother straight out of the gate warmed her heart. "She's already more lucid. I think the IV is helping flush out her system."

"The good news is racking up today," he said with a smile that kicked her heart rate up a few notches. There was something magical and magnetic about his smile. Then again, all sharp angles and planes, she could stare at this man's face all day. Don't even get her started about the depth to his eyes.

"When we get home, I need to check Meg's room to see if any of her papers have been disturbed," she said, not wanting to think too much about the close call with her grandmother. Questions pushed through anyway. Like, what if Birdie had come home alone? Or worse, what if she'd decided to stay a couple of nights at the ranch? It would have been easy to do, especially at Fallon's place.

For a split second, Birdie considered whether or not Meg would be safer at the ranch like Fallon had suggested. She quickly shot down the idea, figuring someone had gotten to her vehicle while parked in front of his house.

Had some creep figured both Birdie and Meg would be dead by now? Even if Birdie had survived the snake—her body rocked a tremor just thinking about it—would she have gotten to Meg in time to stop a killer from poisoning her?

Birdie couldn't go there. Not even hypothetically.

Granted, Meg might not have much time left but Birdie planned to make the most of it.

"Do you want to come inside and sit down?" Birdie asked Fallon.

He nodded and her heart skipped a few more beats with eye contact. But his cell buzzed before he could sit down. He glanced at the screen. "It's Adam. I should take this call."

Birdie nodded but reached out for his free hand, linking their fingers. Having a connection to Fallon kept her panic levels at reasonable levels. He was quickly becoming her lifeline, which was strange because she'd never needed anyone in her life before him. Maybe they could stay friends when this was all said and done?

"Hey," Fallon kept his voice a notch above a whisper as he put the call on speaker.

"Thought you should know that Uncle Keif is going off the rails about his family being interviewed for the crime," Adam explained. "Says Lawler can't come to them every time something happens to someone on our side of the family."

"Is he refusing to cooperate?" Fallon asked.

"No, but he's hot under the collar," Adam continued.

"You would think with what Eric told me about Liv's situation that our uncle would be more than willing to cooperate with an investigation." Fallon didn't bother to hide his frustration. What did the man have to hide this time?

"After being in jail recently, I'm sure he has no desire to go back. And this does look bad for his family," he said. "Plus, he said now the sheriff is just looking for a reason to arrest one of them."

"I've heard nothing but good things about Lawler," Fallon said.

"Depends on which side of the family you're on," Adam quipped.

"That's fair," Fallon agreed. "But then, from what I've heard so far, ours has nothing to hide or be ashamed of."

"You won't get any arguments from me there," Adam said. The line got real quiet. Then came, "I just realized something. They came to the wedding."

"Who?" Fallon asked. He knew in the general sense but he wanted exact names.

"Uncle Keif, Aunt Jackie, and a couple of our cousins. I glanced over and kept an eye on them as they stuck to themselves. But I know I saw the twins, Morgan and Nick," Adam supplied. "I thought they were bringing a peace offering but what if they were there on a spy mission?"

It sounded too bizarre to be true, but Fallon had learned a long time ago not to run anything past his family or the lengths his uncle and father would go to get back at each other.

"That places a few of them at the scene," Fallon said. "We need to get someone inside the house who knows how to sweep for listening devices if Lawler isn't there yet."

"Paine should have some idea what he's looking for," Adam reminded. Their head of security came from a military background. "Hold on."

The line went quiet for a few seconds.

Then, Adam came back. "There. I just sent him a text asking him to get coverage for the guard shack so he can come to the main house."

"You might want to have Lawler send a deputy too. They might be able to lift prints from a device," Fallon pointed out. If he was there, he could help with identifying the most likely spots for a bug. He was too far away and had other priorities at the moment. Plus, he trusted the team at the ranch.

"Right. He does have a long list of people to interview and his deputies are working double time so they can move quickly. I'll have Paine look around without touching anything," Adam said. "If he finds a device, I'll call for Lawler."

"Sounds like a plan." The case would move a whole lot quicker with more hands on deck. "By the way, Dad's about to be released from the hospital."

"Right. He's supposed to come home today," Adam said.

"I just spoke to Mom. Happened to catch her at just the right moment," Fallon explained.

"I'll put this in the group chat," Adam said. "Whenever you're ready, you might want to turn it on. It's a whole lot easier to keep everyone updated. No rush, though. This place can be a lot coming at you all at once."

His brother hit the nail on the head.

"Thanks, bro," he said to Adam. "I'll figure it out and see if I can get on board."

"No rush," Adam stated. He ended the call with the promise of an update should anything about the situation at home change.

Support was one of the best things about being home. During his time in the service, he'd bonded with his unit. He'd even convinced himself to a degree they were a substitute for his family. In many ways, they had been. But a blood bond ran thick, and Fallon was starting to adjust to the thought of going home. Really going home. To his cabin. To live. Surrounded by the people he cared most about in the world. Ready to step into his role.

Oddly enough, when he thought of being at home, an image of Birdie popped into his thoughts.

"SOUNDS LIKE PROGRESS," Birdie said to Fallon. It wasn't her place to say she was proud of him for calling his mother, even though she was. It wasn't her place to tell him how amazing a person he was, even though it was true. And it certainly wasn't her place to tell him what an amazing friend he was, even though she couldn't imagine doing any of this without him.

Since words failed her, she pushed up to her tiptoes and pressed a tender kiss to those perfect lips of his. All the reasons why she shouldn't be doing this flew out the window the minute he leaned into the kiss. Birdie got lost. Lost in the tenderness of his touch despite his rough hands. Lost in the moment that threatened to consume her in a raging blaze. Lost in the man who was so sexy, so intelligent, so incredible.

In the next second, heat filled the space between them. She grabbed fistfuls of his shirt, trying to anchor herself against the barrage of sensations alighting her body. No one had ever caused this much welcomed chaos in her body. She could only imagine what sex would be like.

Birdie parted her lips for him, teasing his tongue inside her mouth. His hands came up to cup her face. Her breath quickened and her heart thundered. He took a step forward, pinning her back against the wall. She looped her hands around his neck. The move pushed her breasts flush against his chest, where she could feel his heart beating wildly against her.

The sound of squeaky tennis shoes in the hallway signaled someone was coming. Fallon pulled back first, and then locked gazes. The hungry look in his eyes caused her arms to goose bump and heat to swirl low in her stomach. An ache like she'd never known flooded her. Was this what real passion felt like?

They both stood there, chests heaving. And then Fallon's face broke into a wide smile. He shook his head but didn't speak. He didn't need to. The words were written all over that smirk. A sense of accomplishment welled up inside Birdie that she'd had the same effect on him as he had on her. She certainly didn't want to be rowing this boat alone.

The squeaks walked on past. Fallon reached for her hand, and then linked their fingers. Hand in hand, they walked deeper inside Meg's room. She was sleeping, looking peaceful. Her chest moving up and down in a slow, stable rhythm. A machine beeped, reassurance that Meg was going to be fine. Birdie might not have much time left with her grandmother, so she wanted to make the best of every moment. Here this man was, trying to do everything in his power to make that happen. Birdie had to admit that it was nice someone had her back for a change. An annoying voice in the back of her mind picked that moment to ask if she'd ever been willing to let someone in before Fallon. The short answer there was no. But then, she'd never been able to count on a relationship before, either.

Fallon walked to the back wall next to the window, turned around, and brought Birdie against him. Back to chest, his warmth and steady heartbeat comforted her. She also realized from this vantage point they could keep an eye on both the door and Meg at the same time. She figured his military training had kicked in.

She reminded herself not to get too used to this. Soon enough, they would figure out who was behind the rattlesnake and the poisoning attempt. Then, what?

The money Fallon had promised would allow Birdie to stay home during Meg's final months. Great news, right? So why was the thought of Fallon going back to the ranch without her the equivalent of a punch in the solar plexus?

FALLON COULD HOLD Birdie like this forever. Her rumbling stomach reminded him they had other needs, like food. He leaned down and whispered, "I'm sure there's a cafeteria somewhere inside this place. If you want to keep watch over Meg, I can make a food run. Can't promise it'll be edible, though."

"Looking forward to something truly awful," she quipped.

He wasn't kidding about the staying like this forever bit. He'd tried to convince himself that holding her was his attempt to bring comfort to a stressful situation. In truth, the kiss they'd shared had made it impossible for him to be apart from her. He needed the physical connection as much as he sensed she did.

"I promise to offend your tastebuds as much as possible," he teased, thinking how he would rather spend the next couple of hours exploring her instead. Those thoughts needed to be shelved. Birdie was a beautiful woman, inside and out. The care she gave Meg was above and beyond. Her commitment gave him hope there was still a whole lot of good in the world. He'd seen plenty of the dark side of humanity during his years of service. It warmed his heart to know what was happening back home made the sacrifices worth it.

Birdie pushed off him and then stepped aside. He missed her the second she was gone. She moved a chair over to where they'd been standing. This way, she would still have a view of the door.

He fished his cell phone out of his pocket, and handed it over.

"Program your number in here, please," he said as she took the offering.

She punched in her contact information and then blinked up at him. "There you go."

"My phone will be right here in my hand the whole time I'm gone. If you need anything or see anyone who looks suspicious, text or call. I'll be back so fast it'll make your head spin," he said, and meant it. He sent her a text so she would have his info.

"I'll keep my phone in hand, just in case," she said before retrieving hers from her purse.

He didn't want her to need to use it, but he felt a whole lot more comfortable knowing she could contact him at a moment's notice.

Fallon walked out of the room and turned toward the elevator, feeling like he was leaving a piece of his heart behind. It was a strange sensation. One he'd never experienced before meeting Birdie. Despite only knowing her for a matter of hours, she'd become important to him. So much so, he could barely imagine not being in the same room for five minutes.

There'd been a few women in Fallon's past, but none had ever gotten past his first line of defense. There was always something that held him back, always a reason he couldn't seem to get past more than a few dates before he was ready to move on. Until meeting Birdie, he'd believed it had been his fault. That there was something broken inside him that wouldn't allow him to go there with anyone. Not to a place of commitment, or the desire to wake up together every morning, or the desire to rush home to be together every night.

Birdie was different, a game-changer.

Fallon had no idea what that meant exactly, and their lives were complicated. There might not be anything to figure out. She needed to be with Meg. He needed to face the music, go home, and find his place at the ranch.

In another time and place, and under different circumstances, he could see himself falling for someone like Birdie. See where it took them. And yet...impossible situations were his field of expertise. They seemed to follow him wherever he went.

The cafeteria was on the main floor, opposite the lobby. It amounted to a wall of vending machines. Not exactly gourmet but he figured he could piece together enough to keep them both from starving while they waited for Meg's release.

The meal ended up consisting of a pair of ham and cheese subs, chips, and two cans of Coke. His cell buzzed so he set dinner on the closest table and checked the screen. The message came from security with a message that a deputy had shown up and knocked on Meg's door. He'd placed something in the screen door and then left. The item was most likely a business card. Fallon hated the fact they'd missed the deputy. He, no doubt, would want to investigate the house. Possibly even dust for fingerprints.

Fallon called Birdie. She picked up on the first ring.

"Hello," she said in almost a whisper.

"Is there any chance Meg has a spare key outside?" he asked.

"Under the potted plant at the back door," she informed.

"Can you hold for a sec?" he asked.

"Sure," came the response.

Fallon texted the information to Lawler, who in turn confirmed that he sent the message to the local deputy who'd been sent to investigate. When the exchange was finished, he texted his security detail to find the key and assist the deputy in any way necessary.

"It's all taken care of," he said to Birdie once he got back on the line with her. "A deputy is investigating at Meg's as we speak."

"That's fast," she said. The sound of her voice sent a wave of reassurance rushing through him. He didn't realize how on edge he'd been leaving her alone in the room. Knowing she was fine relaxed him more than he should allow. There were other emotions present that he couldn't afford to focus on at present.

He could already feel himself tripping down a dangerous rabbit hole with Birdie.

As he balanced dinner in his arms again, he caught sight of a man around six feet tall wearing slacks, a button-down shirt, and a black cowboy hat walk toward the elevator bank. All Fallon's instincts prickled. William?

13

Meg's eyes blinked open.

"Well, hello there," Birdie said, pushing to standing. She crossed the room and grabbed onto her grandmother's bony fingers. Meg had lost too much weight in the past few months. Now, Birdie would be able to stay home and make sure Meg ate every meal.

Fallon's generosity was beginning to sink in. She had no idea how she would repay him. Suffice it to say that if she ever got her gourmet doughnut shop off the ground, he would be comped for life.

"Hello, my Birdie." Meg smiled as she reached over and ran her fingers down Birdie's face. The familiar greeting brought happy tears to Birdie's eyes.

"How are you feeling?" she asked.

"Pretty good," Meg said as Fallon walked in the room. Her gaze shifted to him as a look of shock—and delight?—overtook her features. "Are you related to Marshall Firebrand?"

"I'm his grandson," Fallon said, walking over to the table

in between visitor's chairs. He set down the items he'd been cradling. He introduced himself to Meg, who smiled widely.

Birdie saw a bead of sweat on his forehead and made a note to ask him about it later.

"I knew your grandfather very well," Meg said, and Birdie could have sworn the woman's cheeks turned red.

"What was he like?" Fallon asked. "Because I have no clue."

The question seemed to catch Meg off guard. Then, she nodded and gave Fallon a look. "He mentioned that he wasn't very close to his grandchildren. I think he was always sorry about that."

Birdie moved to the food, her stomach reminding her just how empty it was. She took a seat, so she could give Meg and Fallon a chance to talk.

"The man I knew was stubborn and hard to get to know," Fallon admitted.

"Isn't it funny how people can have two faces?" Meg noted. "And sometimes we only ever get to see one side of them."

"I'm afraid that I'm a simple person, ma'am," Fallon said.

"Please, don't call me ma'am. It'll make me look over my shoulder for my ex-mother-in-law, and she's been dead for forty years," Meg quipped. It was good to see her sense of humor was back.

"Now, I see where you get your quick wit," Fallon said to Birdie.

She put her hands up in the surrender position. "I take no responsibility for anything that happens or any information that comes out of this room."

Meg had always commented that bad taste in men ran in the family. Her husband had gone out for milk after Birdie's mother was born, and never came back. He'd been a

Merchant Marine and the two had met while he was on leave. Back then, there was no internet to track someone down, so she'd brought up Mari, short for Marigold, on her own. Not an easy task in those days. Birdie had the utmost respect for Meg because of it.

Considering the serious crush—was it a crush or something far more serious?—Birdie had on Fallon, the family curse seemed to be broken. He was genuine and down-to-earth despite being the richest person she would likely ever meet. His family had an amount of money she couldn't even fathom. And yet, he seemed normal. She almost laughed out loud. Fallon Firebrand was anything but normal. There were a whole lot of other adjectives she could use to describe him, though. Smart. Kind. Gorgeous. Sexy. Focused. Generous. He was the total package, which made her question why he was single.

Of course, he was just coming home from being overseas for a very long time. The question she wanted answered was whether or not he did commitments. Again, she needed to rein herself in because the two had barely met despite her heart trying to say otherwise. It was still true. She barely knew him. And the hot chemistry burning between them could burn out without any warning. Where would that leave her?

Hadn't her mother described her relationship with Birdie's father in the same way? And then there was Meg. Her most successful relationship to date happened with a married man. Granted, his wife had died at some point but Marshall Firebrand's family had no idea who Meg was.

Maybe Birdie's feelings for Fallon were setting her up for the family curse.

She finished her meal and then tuned back into the conversation happening between Meg and Fallon. He needed to eat, so she handed him a sub. He polished it off in no time. It was probably nothing more than a snack for him.

Rather than keep going down the non-relationship track, she shifted gears to what she knew so far about the investigation. A lot had happened in the past few hours. There were multiple investigations ongoing. The one at the Firebrand Ranch involved multiple interviews happening. At Meg's house, a deputy was dusting for prints. The law enforcement officer would most likely canvas the neighborhood.

The forward motion felt good, but not better than the thought of having the freedom to be with Meg. Birdie could cry for what a godsend Fallon had been. The other Firebrands seemed nice enough too. At least that was true for the ones she'd met so far. And yet, there was something special about him. She couldn't imagine anyone else being willing to put their own life on hold to help a virtual stranger. He'd said it was what ranchers did. She hoped there was more to it than that. On that note, Birdie realized she needed to get serious. The reason she'd never dated anyone like Fallon was because a man like him had the power to shatter her heart into a thousand tiny pieces. Into flecks of dust so small they couldn't be seen by the naked eye.

"I owe you a game of blackjack," Meg said when Birdie tuned back into their conversation.

"Hold on a minute," Fallon said. "How do I know you're not a card shark?"

"You don't." Meg slapped her knee and laughed. It was a musical sound. One Birdie heard far too little of since the diagnosis. "But I'll take your money either way."

"Can I ask a serious question?" Fallon asked after a pause.

"Shoot," Meg said. She seemed to realize the gravity of the situation because she sat up a little bit straighter. She clasped her hands together and leaned in toward Fallon, like she was hanging on every word.

"What was the Marshall really like?" he asked.

"That's easy." Meg lit up. "He knew how to treat a lady, for one. He always brought a gift when he came. And flowers. He would send the biggest bouquet you ever saw whenever we were on again."

"Can I ask why you guys went back and forth? Why not stay together and try to make it work?" he asked.

"He thought it would upset his kids to see him with another woman besides their mother," she admitted. "Between you, me, and the fence post, there was more to it than that. I don't think he ever got over losing her." Meg's tone was wistful now. "He had a lot of regrets about the way he treated her during their marriage. I don't think he ever thought he deserved such a wonderful person. He was very hard on himself."

"He sure came off as confident around us," he said. Fallon leaned forward, resting his elbows on his knees, hands clasped. He seemed rapt.

"Bull-hockey," Meg quipped. "Oh, I don't doubt a child would have a hard time seeing right through him, but he never fooled me. Do you know about his own father?"

Fallon shook his head and the look on his face struck Birdie. She could only imagine how much this piece of his personal history meant to him. It was innate in a person to want to know where they came from, their family.

"The man was pure evil," she said. "Marshall didn't like to talk about him much. But there were times when he couldn't help himself."

"What did he say?" Fallon asked.

"Did you ever see your grandfather's back?" she asked. "Did he ever take his shirt off in front of you?"

"No." Fallon's forehead creased and his eyebrow shot up. "Not that I can remember."

"Did you ever see him go swimming or accidentally walk in on him while he was getting out of the shower?" she continued.

"Nothing like that," Fallon said.

Birdie's heart dropped. So much about a person was made up of broken pieces from their past. Fallon was strong and had such a need to find his own identity. She respected him so much for that.

"I probably should stop right here then." Meg compressed her lips and Fallon frowned.

"IT WOULD MEAN a lot if you kept going." Fallon wanted to know more about the Marshall. Yet, he didn't want Meg to feel compromised. "I understand if you can't."

She sat there for a long moment before looking to Birdie and asking for a sip of water.

Was she stalling for time? The IV fluids should make her want to float away by now.

Meg picked up the large plastic water container and handed it to Meg. She brought the straw to her mouth, barely sipped. After returning the drink to the table, she exhaled.

"Marshall had a strict upbringing with high expectations. He was supposed to be a doctor or lawyer, not a rancher, even though ranching was the family business." Meg flashed eyes at Fallon. "I'm not making excuses, mind you."

Fallon leaned back, and listened while Meg took the floor. His understanding of the brokenness of his grandfather multiplied with every piece of information Meg shared.

"The tiniest mistake and his father would make him kneel for hours on end," she said. "He admitted to having a rebellious spirit, so his knees got a lot of work."

Fallon could identify there. He'd never liked being told what to do.

Meg toyed with the edge of her blanket where the fabric folded over, creating a corner.

"But the beatings were the worst." She looked up at Fallon and then diverted her eyes. "And they happened a lot. Marshall took the brunt of them for his mother and younger brother too."

"I didn't know the Marshall had a younger brother." This was news to Fallon. More surprises from a man who'd spent a lifetime holding his cards to his chest. To be fair, it wasn't like he was close to his grandfather. The only thing he was beginning to see was how lonely the man's life must have been. "Wouldn't there be pictures around of him? Phone calls?"

"Oh," Meg said.

Fallon would bet money there was a story behind the secret brother. He could see the discomfort in Meg at feeling like she might be breaking confidences. "I'd like to know more, if that's okay. It's helping me understand a person who has been a mystery to me for most of my life."

"Okay." She paused a few beats. "When Marshall was in a mood, I always knew he was thinking about his brother," Meg admitted. "Marshall went to a very dark place."

"Did he ever tell you what happened?" Fallon asked.

"Only that Marshall couldn't get his brother to the

hospital in time. He'd been whipped by their father to within an inch of his life," she said.

"Why not call the law?" he asked.

"Times were different back then." She shrugged. "The law didn't get involved in family affairs, unless someone was willing to file charges."

She took in a slow breath before continuing.

"Clive, that was his name, eventually decided he'd had enough. A few weeks later and in a fit of anger, he marched into the barn and grabbed the first thing he could find. Marshall believed his brother was only trying to make a point, not take his own life. He got hold of a jug of cyanide that had been stored in the barn and used to get rid of rabbits." Meg wiped a stray tear. "Marshall always blamed himself for not being there to stop his brother. He was the one who used to calm Clive down after a fight with their father. Marshall said his brother didn't have the same thick skin he did. Said he took things personally. Marshall lost his best friend and confidant. After that, I believe he just hardened in order to survive."

"Thank you for telling me this, Meg." Fallon might never know the Marshall, but this explained a lot about him and why he might push his own sons to be 'stronger' through competition with each other. The tactic wasn't right by any means, but Fallon had a better understanding.

"I have no idea what Marshall was like with you or your family. Sounds like he was a different person with me," she admitted. "But I always knew he had secrets. In fact, I didn't know he was married until after I'd fallen for him. How's that for being young and naïve on my part?"

"How long were you dating before you figured it out?" Curiosity got the best of him, so he asked the question knowing full well she might not be willing to answer.

"Years," she said before throwing her hands up in the air. "It sounds so cliché now but he came to one of my shows. I was young and had my daughter, who was barely old enough to walk. Between my daughter and my work, I didn't have a lot of time for men. I was still hurting." She flashed eyes at him and he quickly realized she didn't want to discuss that particular part of her past. "The gallery owner introduced us. We ended up talking for hours. Things happened from there. Marshall would show up with flowers and presents. I never knew when he would be at my door. I guess that was part of the excitement of it all."

Fallon smiled at watching how her eyes sparkled at the memory.

"He could be quite charming," she admitted, clasping her hands together and bringing them to her heart. "We saw each other every few months and, to be honest, I didn't ask a whole lot of questions. I didn't want to be attached to anyone else, the way I'd been with—"

A knock sounded at the door. A nurse walked in with a wheelchair.

"Are you ready to get out of here?" she asked.

Meg clapped. The twinkle returned to her eyes. "Are those my discharge papers?"

"Yes, ma'am." The nurse picked up the clipboard from the seat of the wheelchair.

"I'll wait out in the hallway," Fallon said, realizing Meg would need to get dressed. He glanced at Birdie before walking out.

As he stood at the doorway, he thought about what Meg had just told him. It was difficult to see the Marshall as just a man. And even harder to imagine him as the scared young boy he must have been. He'd been larger than life to Fallon growing up. Still was in many respects. The same went for Fallon's father. This new light changed things.

He pulled out his cell phone and loaded the app his brother had mentioned. An invitation popped up almost immediately. The group read, Firebrand.

Fallon took in a deep breath, and then accepted the invite.

14

"There's no place like home." Meg beamed.

Fallon wondered if he'd ever feel that way about a place as he helped Meg inside her bungalow. He was from the ranch but that didn't mean much. Overseas had always been a temporary stop. The best hope for him was his cabin.

It was late. Lights were out in neighboring houses. He would have to wait until morning to knock on doors.

"Let's just take her straight to bed," Birdie said. There was a quality to her voice he couldn't quite pinpoint that made her feel a lot like home.

Fallon mentally shook off the thought, stopping in front of the bedroom door.

"Can you take it from here?" he asked Birdie.

"I got this," she confirmed.

While Birdie helped Meg get ready for bed, he could get a briefing from his security detail. He highly doubted a local deputy would allow one of Fallon's people to accompany him on an investigation. Hopefully, he could get some information. And then there was Adam and the group chat.

Fallon stepped out front as he texted, requesting one of the security members to meet him out front. He sat down on the steps of the small porch as he heard the van door open then close. A woman who couldn't be more than five feet two inches approached.

"Sir," she said. Her brown hair was pulled back in a ponytail. She walked like a cop, and he wondered if she worked as a police officer somewhere in her background. The security firm she worked for was the best. He wouldn't be surprised at all if she'd been SWAT or an MP in her past.

"What do you have?" he asked, getting straight to the point.

"A man wearing a deputy's uniform arrived at approximately o-five-hundred." She pulled out her cell phone and brought up a picture. "Deputy Barton's identity checked out, so my colleague gave him the instructions to retrieve a key located behind a plant at the back door. Deputy Barton proceeded to inspect the home. He examined medication bottles and took several pictures in order to locate a fingerprint. He did not say whether or not he was successful, sir."

"Did he canvas the neighbors?" Fallon asked.

"Yes, sir," she confirmed. "We were requested to stay in our vehicle during this time."

Not a surprise.

"Did anyone else approach the home?" he asked, but whoever was behind this had to know they were onto them.

"No, sir," she confirmed. "There was no one in the cul-de-sac either. A Buick Regal left this residence," she pointed across the street from Meg's, "at approximately o-two-hundred-hours, returning one hour later. There was no sign of interest in the van or the residence we've been assigned to monitor."

"Thank you," Fallon said, figuring the investigation

would take time. In the meantime, the jerk responsible needed to make a mistake. One mistake was all Fallon needed to catch the sonofa— "You're dismissed."

"Thank you, sir."

While he was outside and still had his phone in hand, he figured he might as well give Adam a call. His brother picked up on the first ring.

"Hey, I was fixing to call you with an update," Adam said right away.

"Good timing," Fallon said. "What do you have?"

"Lawler said there were no fingerprints on Birdie's vehicle," Adam said.

"None other than hers, right?" he asked.

"Not exactly. The passenger door handle had been wiped clean," Adam informed.

"Which means someone didn't want to leave a trail," Fallon said. "And proves this was calculated."

"Paine said one of his guys reported a suspicious person on property. The person took off into the woods," Adam continued. "He had on camo, so he blended right in once he got into the trees. Paine was working on the report."

"I'm guessing our guy didn't get close enough to get a description," Fallon said.

"That's affirmative," Adam agreed.

"Do you think one of our family members could be responsible?" Fallon asked.

"In all honesty, I don't even want to consider the possibility," Adam said. "Considering the fact someone bugged the main house—"

"Has that been confirmed?" Fallon asked.

"Afraid so," Adam stated.

"Which narrows down the possibilities of who could be involved," Fallon said. "There were only a handful of family members who have been near the main house recently. The ones you mentioned who showed up at the wedding."

"We were hoping that was a goodwill gesture," Adam said, disappointment in his tone.

"Lawler will most likely focus on them as he pursues a family angle," Fallon said.

"They, unfortunately, have the most to gain from discounting the will," Adam agreed. "That gives them motive. Aunt Jackie is freaking out about the possibility of her husband being arrested again."

"I'm not trying to oversimplify the problem here, but wouldn't it be a whole lot easier if we just found a way to make everyone happy with this inheritance?" Fallon asked. "Couldn't we do some type of drawing or just split everything down the middle like it probably should be in the first place?"

"I've considered it a dozen times. That would be up to Dad and Uncle Keif to decide," Adam pointed out. "And, second, have you tried getting half of us in a room and agreeing on something as simple as what to have for lunch?"

No, he hadn't. Not recently. "I guess it's too much to hope that everyone has grown up and would be willing to work things through instead of fighting."

"There's a whole lot of us, and a whole lot of strong opinions," Adam stated. He would know. He'd stayed on to work the ranch from day one. His big brother had always known his place in life. He'd always felt a draw toward the land and carrying on the family legacy. "How's it going on your end?"

Fallon gave a quick update on the mystery visitor, the medication, and the trip to the hospital.

"Turns out, Birdie's grandmother has been in an on-again, off-again relationship with the Marshall for longer than we've been alive," Fallon added at the end of his update.

"That means our grandmother was still around," Adam surmised.

"Yes," Fallon confirmed. He gave a brief history of the affair. "Did the Marshall ever talk to you about his childhood?"

"Me?" The shock in Adam's voice answered for him. He chuckled. "I don't even know the man's favorite kind of beer."

"Is it strange to you that he's gone?" Fallon asked, figuring his brother had been around the Marshall a whole more than him.

"It happened so fast," Adam stated. "We were all caught off guard."

"The news came out of nowhere," Fallon agreed. "I just thought we had...I don't know...time."

"Same here, bro," Adam said. "What's catching me the most off guard is the situation with Dad."

"Have you been by to see him now that he's home?" Fallon asked.

"To be honest, I've been busy with the investigation," Adam said. "Then, there's my daughter, who is keeping me hopping. I never knew someone so small could have so many needs."

Adam's tone lightened considerably when he spoke about Angel.

"That's another face punch," Fallon said with a chuckle. "Gotta admit. You and fatherhood? I didn't see that one coming."

Adam laughed too.

"When I get home, we should have a beer together," Fallon said to his brother.

"I'd like that a lot," Adam said.

The door opened behind him and Birdie stepped onto the porch. She saw that he was on the phone and immediately stepped back.

"I'll be inside," she whispered.

He waved her to come out before ending the call with his brother.

"That was Adam," he said, motioning for her to take a seat beside him.

She sat so close the outer part of her thighs touched. More of that electricity shot through him with the contact. He liked the familiar jolt. He reached for her hand and then linked their fingers.

BIRDIE LEANED into Fallon as he brought her up to speed on his phone call with Adam.

"Your family must be furious," she said.

"And feeling betrayed," he admitted. "No one wants to believe a Firebrand could be responsible for any of this."

"I'm sure everyone has already thought of this, but others could be responsible," she pointed out. "There's no telling how long those bugs have been planted."

"Very true," he said with a slight nod before asking about Meg.

"I'm pretty sure she was snoring before I left the room. I checked around to see if anything else had been disturbed. A few drawers were open. Someone was definitely in the house searching for the will. It's the only thing that makes any sense," she informed.

"The deputy wouldn't have opened drawers," he said. "The fingerprints were wiped from your passenger's side door. I'm guessing the person responsible didn't leave any behind here either."

"Couldn't be the same person. They would have had to be in two places at one time," she reasoned.

"Exactly. Someone has a network. Resources," he agreed. "Fingers are pointing toward the other side of my family."

"It makes sense based on what I know about what's at stake and who stands to gain the most," she said. "Killing me and Meg won't make this go away now."

"Do you have the original document in your possession?" he asked.

She nodded.

"Good. The pictures Adam took wouldn't be defensible in court. The person behind this would want to destroy the original document and anyone attached to it."

"And that is?" she asked.

"My side of the family inherits the land and cattle. Their side of the family inherits mineral rights," he said.

"What about money?" she asked.

"There are trusts set up. No one is broke, but the rub is that Uncle Keif can't drill on the property without the land owner's permission, which means he has to work something out with my father. The two have been going at it their entire lives. No one expects them to suddenly make peace now," he said. "Plus, for some, there's no amount of money that will make them happy. They will always want more."

"So, basically, it's just going to be who ends up with more zeroes in a bank account?" she asked. "That's the endgame?"

"It appears so," he said. "For the record, that is definitely not how I feel about life."

"You left all that behind to serve your country, Fallon. I don't think you should ever doubt your priorities," she said.

He squeezed her hand, and all kinds of electric impulses vibrated through her.

"I'm not saying it's the right way to go about it, but it almost seems like your grandfather wanted his sons to get along after all," she said.

"Before meeting Meg, I would have laughed at anyone who said those words. Now? I'm inclined to agree," he said. "He might be trying to accomplish in death what he never could in life...peace between his sons."

"From everything you said, the divide between brothers runs deep," she pointed out.

The two of them sat there for a long moment in comfortable silence, and she realized there was no other place she'd rather be than right here, right now with Fallon.

"Based on what I've heard about your grandfather, he sounds like he was set in his ways," Birdie finally said. "He obviously changed the will recently. I wonder when that happened?"

"Good question," he said. "Our family attorney should know something about the timeline. That might help."

"Might be worth giving him a call to see when he last changed the document," she said, figuring he could map the date to what was going on with the family at the time of the change.

"I haven't spoken to Harlen Sawyer in more years than I can count," Fallon said, picking up his cell phone.

"Is it too late to call?" she asked. Office hours must be closed at this point.

"Harlen is on speed dial when it comes to my family," he said.

Of course, he was. Birdie still couldn't wrap her mind around the kind of money that put security vans outside people's houses on a moment's notice or had a family lawyer available on a moment's notice.

Based on the fact Fallon had ditched everything he knew for the military, she assumed he'd never developed a comfort level with his upbringing. At first, she'd wondered why on earth someone would turn their back on being rich. It had always seemed like a golden ticket to Birdie. Now? Not so much.

15

"Fallon Firebrand. I heard you were home," Harlen said after biting back a yawn.

"News travels fast." Fallon was beginning to realize just how fast.

"Are you back for the long haul?" Harlen asked.

"That's the idea," Fallon said.

"Welcome home," Harlen said. There was that word again. Strangely, with Birdie at his side, it was beginning to fit.

"Thank you," Fallon said. He'd never been one to mince words, so he decided to get right to the point. "Sorry to wake you—"

"No worries, Fallon. You know that," he said.

"I'm not sure if Sheriff Lawler reached out to you yet but, if not, you should expect a call," Fallon continued before giving Harlen a quick rundown. "Which brings me to my question. When did the Marshall last change his will?"

"I don't have the exact date." The sound of a light being flipped on and the ruffle of a bedspread came through the line. "I could turn on my computer—"

"How about a timeframe? Was it last year? Two years ago? So long ago you can't remember?" Fallon wanted to put it in perspective and create a timeline as best he could.

"Oh, that's easy. A year and a half ago," Harlen stated with pride in his voice. "I remember because it was somewhere close to the beginning of calf season when your grandfather mentioned he wanted a new will. I thought he was losing his mind. I don't have to remind you how busy that time of year is."

"Brings back all kinds of bad memories trying to get homework done, play sports, and help out at the ranch," Fallon admitted. "Did the Marshall ever say why he suddenly needed the will changed?"

"You know your grandfather," Harlen said. "He wasn't asking for advice. He'd made up his mind and he wanted it done right then."

"He did have a habit of snapping his fingers and expecting everyone to jump," Fallon agreed.

"When I asked him why the sudden change, he said he didn't expect to live forever," Harlen said. "Naturally, I asked him if there was something wrong with him. If he'd been to the doctor. Got a diagnosis that I should know about."

Fallon could guess the answers to those questions, considering the Marshall had died in a freak accident through no fault of his own.

"He told me to mind my own business and my job. Then, he threatened to fire me if I didn't." Harlen laughed. "I've been the family attorney forty years, and he threatens my job if I don't shut up and pull together the will."

"Why didn't you put the clause in there that cancels out any previous wills, Harlen?" Fallon asked. It wasn't like him to make a mistake.

"I'll tell you the honest truth," he said. "I felt like he was being coerced. He'd cut out a person who had been very important to him and it didn't seem right."

Harlen had left a legal door open? Was that person Meg?

"Do you have any ideas who might have been coercing him into changing his mind?" Fallon asked.

"I couldn't get a name out of him and there was no way I could ask outright," he admitted. "I just couldn't see him leaving out a person he'd been close to and had insisted be part of every will I've ever drafted for the man since he hired me forty years ago."

It had to be Meg. Harlen was protecting her name.

"I'll say one thing, though," Harlen lowered his voice like he was about to spill a secret. "I'd look to who had the most to gain from the changes."

"That would be my uncle and his side of the family," Fallon admitted.

"You might want to check Marshall's calendar," Harlen said. "It's probably too late for phone records but he might have logged some of his activities."

"The Marshall online?" Fallon asked.

"Desk calendar," Harlen said. "And, no, your grandfather wouldn't even own a computer if he didn't absolutely have to."

Fallon thanked the family attorney for the information before ending the call. He figured it was too late to call one of his brothers. Until he remembered the group text room. He could put the information out there and ask someone to check out the Marshall's desk first thing in the morning. He pulled up the app and started typing. Then, he realized his mother was in the group and decided against the text.

There were recent messages in the group, though. Fallon opened the app. The most recent one read: *Yelling can be heard from Uncle Keif's place. Aunt Jackie is on a terror.*

Rather than blast a message to the group, he sent a private text to Adam. He could read it when he got up in a few hours. Speaking of which, Birdie had yawned three times during his call with Harlen. Fallon wouldn't mind closing his eyes for a quick rest.

"Where do you want me?" he asked Birdie, who'd been quiet while she sat next to him. Her quick smile followed by a rush of heat to her cheeks had him adding, "To sleep."

"Right." She pushed up to standing and he immediately noticed all the warmth went with her despite the still hot temperatures. "Follow me."

He did, locking the door behind them. It was something he couldn't fathom doing at home until the recent spate of crimes against his family. Half the beauty of small-town life was the fact he could leave his keys in his truck if he wanted to. He could even keep it running if all he had to do was run into the feed store or the post office back in the day.

Time stood still for no one, him included. He was slowly adjusting to the reality of life outside the military and all the changes that had taken place while he was out of the country.

"The bathroom is across the hall," Birdie whispered. "There's only one but the water pressure is good in the shower."

"Sounds good. I can make myself comfortable in the second recliner," he said. "I'm good with a couple of hours."

"Would you mind sleeping in my bed?" she asked, and then seemed to hear how that could be interpreted. "I'm only thinking that I don't want to scare Meg if she wakes in the middle of the night and stumbles into the kitchen. I have no idea what she'll remember when she wakes up."

"Where will you sleep?" he asked.

"It's a king-sized bed. I can stick to my side," she said.

"Shame," he said low and under his breath before agreeing to the arrangement. He retrieved his rucksack and then dropped it off in Birdie's bedroom while she took the first shift in the shower. He did his level best to force his thoughts away from the fact she was naked in the room across the hall.

Thankfully, she was out in ten minutes. He took a turn, cutting her time in half. What could he say? Real showers were a luxury where he'd been, and he was trained to hop in and get out. Plus, the thought of spending the night with Birdie had stirred his heart.

"I CAN PUT pillows in between us, but I promise not to bite, Birdie said to Fallon."

He mumbled something that sounded a whole lot like the word, *shame.*

A dozen butterflies released in her stomach as she saw a shirtless Fallon. The man's muscles had muscles. There were a lot of scars too that made her want to reach out to him, hold him.

"Don't worry about pillows," he said. "I won't take up much room."

She must have shot him a look because he broke into a wide smile.

"I'm a side sleeper," he clarified.

"Good, because I can't imagine that body not taking up space." Birdie heard how that sounded coming out of her mouth. She clamped those loose lips shut. Then, she pointed to his side.

She hadn't slept with anyone in the same bed since her relationship with Ethan ended almost a year ago.

"I don't usually sleep with women," Fallon said. "The guys in my unit tell me that I snore."

"So, you only sleep with men?" she teased.

"Oh, I've slept with plenty..." Again, he laughed. "I'm just going to stop right there before I say something else I might regret."

"Are you saying that you don't do 'sleepovers' with women?" She probably shouldn't ask the question because she most likely didn't want to know the answer. And yet, there she was, asking away.

"As a matter of fact, I don't," he stated, and his serious tone goose bumped her arms. She told herself not to ask about that later.

The right side of the bed dipped underneath his weight. For a split second she imagined how good he would feel, skin-to-skin. Birdie sighed sharply, and gave herself a mental headshake. Pining for the man sitting next to her in bed wouldn't make sleep come any faster. And she was tired. So tired.

Still, the air in the room charged with electricity. Birdie might have flipped the light switch off, but she was suddenly wide awake. The sound of Fallon's even breathing comforted her, but his clean spicy scent awakened every uniquely feminine part of her.

So, yeah, she was not going to be able to sleep next to this gorgeous man no matter how tired she'd been two minutes ago. And that just made her want to laugh.

"Are you awake?" Fallon's voice was so quiet she almost didn't hear him.

"Yes," she whispered.

"What I said before about not spending the night with women," he began. She didn't want to think about him in bed with another person at this moment. "I've never wanted to wake up with someone next to me before."

"Are you saying you've never been in a long-term relationship?" she asked. He'd told her that he'd signed up in the service two years after high school and hadn't been home since. Was it even possible that he'd never been committed to anyone? Or was there a 'special' person in every port?

"I have," he said. "But I've never spent the whole night. It just never seemed all that important to me before. The relationships that I've been in seemed content to take what I could give. No one asked for more."

"And when they ended?" she asked.

"There were never any hurt feelings," he said. "I was honest about what I was capable of giving with a job like mine. I never wanted to be one of those soldiers who slept with a picture of his girlfriend or wife. Or worse...kids. I never wanted someone lying awake at night wondering if I was ever coming home or dreading the sound of every knock at the door thinking that it might be a military officer and a chaplain. I just didn't think it would be fair to do that to another person."

"Hasn't there been anyone who made you want to hold onto them or figure it out together?" she asked quietly.

"No."

"Why are you telling me this, Fallon?" Was this some kind of warning not to get involved with him? Because as much as her mind said no, her heart seemed to have other ideas. It caused her hand to reach out to touch his arm. He immediately found her hand and linked their fingers.

"I wanted you to know that I don't normally do this," he said before bringing her hand up to his mouth and feathering a kiss on her palm.

"But we aren't dating, Fallon." Birdie had no idea why she'd pointed out the fact.

"Shame," he said a little louder than before.

"Even if we wanted to, I don't see how it would work out," Birdie continued. She was already on the track. She might as well finish the race.

"I've been thinking the same thing," he admitted.

The fact he'd been considering how a relationship between them might go blew her mind. Was it too much to hope they could magically figure it out?

"I have responsibilities here with Meg." Birdie figured she needed to get the obvious out of the way first. An annoying voice in the back of her mind said she was running scared. Part of her always believed what Meg said about their family being cursed when it came to relationships.

"I'll be moving into my home at the ranch," he said, and it was almost like all hope had burst in those few moments. "Trying to settle into my new life."

"The hours will be long for both of us," she said.

"They will," he agreed. "There's a whole lot going on at the ranch that I'll need to be brought up to speed on."

"What about days off?" she asked.

He laughed. "From what I remember about ranching, those are far and few between."

"I'm needed here with Meg," Birdie said. The annoying voice returned, saying those were circumstances. But they were real life, she corrected. Real responsibilities. Real commitments that were being made to others that couldn't be taken back because they weren't convenient anymore.

Wow. Had she really just had that whole conversation in her head. Because the annoying voice responded with one word...*excuses*.

Birdie had never believed in the whole *love conquers all* fairy tale.

"Birdie?" Fallon asked. She loved hearing her name roll off his tongue.

"Yes?" she responded as her pulse kicked up a few notches.

"It's a shame, isn't it," he said with a sleepy voice that threatened to break down all her carefully constructed walls.

She didn't respond. Couldn't respond. Because here was a perfect man in bed right next to her and all she could think about was how much she was going to be shattered when he walked out the door.

Why did it always come down to that?

16

Fallon rubbed his eyes and yawned. The sun peaked through slats in the miniblinds. The minute he moved, Birdie rolled over onto her side. She propped herself up on one elbow.

"Morning." Her sleepy voice was all kinds of sexy, but he couldn't let himself slide down the slippery slope of magically wishing their lives were somehow different, and that they'd be able to figure out a way to make it work. Some people might accuse him of not trying hard enough, but he'd tried to force relationships in the past and none had turned out the way he'd expected or hoped.

"Hey," he said, bringing his finger up to run along her jawbone. Touching Birdie was the worst of bad ideas. Skin-to-skin contact, no matter how many clothes he had on, caused all kinds of sensations in his body.

"I can't believe I actually slept last night," she said. Looking into those autumn eyes of hers wasn't helping with the attraction a bit.

"Yeah, same." He rolled over, and then pushed off the bed. His morning breath needed to be checked. He threw on a shirt, grabbed his toiletry bag from his rucksack, and made his way across the hall.

Since Meg's room was right next door to the bathroom and the walls were paper thin, he could hear snoring. He took it as a good sign she was catching up on rest. The medication switch yesterday had most likely taken a toll on her body. She could sleep for the better part of the day.

Fallon heard Birdie getting out of bed across the hall. Was it a big mistake to get out of bed without telling her how he felt? He'd approached the subject last night but she'd kept her head on straight, whereas he was thinking with his heart. Maybe it was better for him to go home once Birdie and Meg were safe, get his bearings, and then see where they stood in a few months. Logic said that would be the best route. It would give them both time to get their lives in order.

Plus, Birdie had been right about this being the worst possible time in their lives to try to start up a new relationship. Relationships needed time. He'd seen plenty of his dwindle before they even got started because he would have to ship out on a moment's notice. He'd barely had time to shoot off a text before some missions. Others, he got no notice at all and his relationships suffered as a result.

There were a few heartbreaks along the way. There'd been a couple of people he could see going long-term. All had ended in the same manner with almost the exact same message. He didn't have time to give to a real relationship.

By the time he returned to Birdie's room, she was dressed and ready to trade rooms. The sound of her splashing water on her face and then brushing her teeth shouldn't tug at his heart in the way it did. Why was something so basic taking on a meaning? An annoying voice in the back of his head reminded him that he never stuck around for morning rituals. No arguing there.

Birdie returned looking fresh-faced and even more beautiful. No one should look that good in shorts, a t-shirt that fit in all the right places, and a tied off lightweight flannel. She pushed up to her tiptoes and gave him a peck on the lips but it could have been a full-on kiss for the effect it had. Liquid heat boiled in his veins and it took all his willpower to stop himself from hauling her against his chest. The thought of her body moving against his under those sheets was enough to send him to a cold shower if he didn't cut it out.

Fallon retrieved his cell phone and checked the screen.

"I'll put on coffee," Birdie said as a knock sounded at the front door.

"Food delivery," Fallon said, glancing at his texts.

"I'm on it," she said.

"I'll be right there." A message in the group text caught his attention. He sat on the edge of the bed as he read it. A few choice words slipped out before he could rein them in. This time, he called Eric.

"I'm guessing you read the message," Eric said after a quick greeting.

"Lawler found listening equipment in Uncle Keif's garage," Fallon said. "I haven't been around the man in more years than I care to count, but despite that, there's still no way I would pin him for attempted murder."

"It's circumstantial evidence but having that in his workshop doesn't exactly look good," Eric noted. "Although, he swears up and down the equipment doesn't belong to him. He also said he never goes in the workshop anymore."

"What does Lawler have to say about that?" Fallon asked.

"There's dust on his tools and his workbench, so he could be telling the truth," Eric informed.

"What do you think?" Fallon asked.

"The same as you probably do. This looks suspect," Eric said. He issued a sharp sigh. "But then, would he really be this stupid? He was already arrested and released with a harassment case pending against him for his actions with Liv."

"What about Kellan?" Fallon asked. Their cousin was the oldest out of everyone and he seemed to want to make certain everyone knew it while growing up together.

"It would be stupid for him to pull something like this," Eric said.

"Not at his own home," Fallon pointed out.

"After what happened, I have a hard time believing he would want to bring down more heat on his father. Kellan was a wreck when his father was in jail. He's still licking his wounds from losing Liv. I do believe he had deep feelings for her," Eric explained.

"Okay then, what about the others? The twins came to the wedding," Fallon remembered.

"This is the tricky part. Who wants to believe any of our family members would be capable of attempted murder?" Eric asked.

"I sure don't. I might have been away for a long time but I sure didn't expect to come home to find such division in our family," Fallon stated. "I spoke to Harlen Sawyer last night."

"Really?" Eric asked.

"He said the will was updated eighteen months ago and that he didn't put a clause in the current will on purpose because he believed the Marshall was being influenced by someone," Fallon said. "He also mentioned the will cut out someone who had been very special to him."

"Interesting," Eric stated, and it sounded like the wheels were already turning.

"He thought it might be a good idea to grab the Marshall's desk calendar to see if he wrote down who he was spending time with that we might have missed," Fallon said. "Of course, if the man hid his relationship with Meg from literally everyone, he might not have written a name down."

"It's worth checking into. Romy is in there working now. I'll go into his office and dig around. See what I can find," Eric said.

"Let me know if anything turns up," Fallon said.

"You got it," Eric said without hesitation. "Eighteen months ago would have put the changes to the will around calving season."

"That's right," Fallon said. "It's the reason Harlen thought the timing was suspect."

"He makes a good point there," Eric agreed. Calving season consumed their lives between health checks, births, logging, and tagging. There was a whole mess of paperwork involved. Most folks didn't realize how much paperwork was involved in ranching. All they had was the image of a cowboy riding the range at sunset. What would be considered the least cool parts by most consumed a whole lot of time, paperwork and checking fences. Keeping proper fences held cattle within bounds and inside safe territory. It also made them harder to steal.

Fallon updated his brother on the mystery guest who'd gone through Meg's personal things, no doubt searching for the original copy of the will.

"I'll check it out now and get back to you," Eric said before ending the call.

The finger kept pointing to Uncle Keif's side of the family. Maybe the Marshall's calendar would reveal who should be hauled in for questioning. His instincts said Uncle Keif wasn't responsible. After all the heat that had been brought down on him after the Liv case—a case that was still pending—he'd be stupid to set up a listening device in his garage workshop to spy on the main house. Of course, it might be exactly the kind of thing an innocent person would do to get a feel for what was happening. What did he hope to gain?

Next, Fallon checked in with his security detail. Not much had happened since their meeting last night. After breakfast and coffee, he figured he could canvas the neighbors. He checked his watch. Most country folk he knew got up and moving before the sun.

He checked his e-mail, noting the schedule for today. An aide would be by around eight a.m. to check on Meg. He made note of the nurse's aides who would be stopping by throughout the day to entertain Meg and help her with whatever she needed or wanted, copying his security detail on the timing of visits and what to expect. Food had already been delivered, so that would get them through the next couple of days without needing to cook. Birdie was most likely putting the pre-made meals and groceries away as he ran through the details. Then, there was the housekeeping service, who would arrive after lunch.

Once Fallon had a good handle on what to expect, he walked into the kitchen to the smell of dark roast brewing.

"This is too much," Birdie said as she heard him shuffling in. She opened the fridge door and waved a hand like she was in a showroom presenting a new car.

His chest swelled with pride at the smile on her face. With all the supplies they could ever need at their disposal and a security detail parked outside, Fallon wasn't technically needed here. And yet, he couldn't bring himself to think about leaving.

"You're amazing. Thank you." Birdie closed the fridge door and immediately stepped closer to Fallon. She popped up on her tiptoes and pressed another kiss to his lips. This was dangerous territory and she knew it. Stopping herself was a whole different story. She knew what she wanted and went for it. Would there be a price to pay later? The answer was most likely a hard yes.

Birdie ignored the thought, figuring that having this moment would be worth the pain later.

"I sent over the schedule for today," he said, looping his arms around her waist. He dipped his head down and claimed her lips with a little more intensity this time.

Fireworks went off inside her chest.

She broke apart when the coffee machine beeped. He beat her to the pot, grabbing one of the mugs she'd set out, filling it, and then handing it over. Then, he poured one for himself.

"What sounds good to eat?" she asked after taking a sip and enjoying the burn on her throat. "We have breakfast tacos—"

"You had me at breakfast," he said with a smile that lit all kinds of fires inside her.

"Tacos it is." She took another sip before pulling out a container. She plated and then microwaved the dishes. The room filled with an amazing scent. Not quite as good as

Fallon's clean and spicy scent, but that would be near-impossible to beat.

Fallon took the plates from her and helped set the table. She could get used to having this man around. Another dangerous thought.

"I spoke to my brother a few minutes ago," he said as they sat down at the table to eat.

"I thought I heard you speaking to someone," she said.

"The sheriff found listening equipment at my uncle Keif's house," Fallon stated.

Birdie gasped.

"Seriously?" she asked.

"Eric is checking on the Marshall's desk calendar," he stated before taking a bite. "Said he'd call as soon as he got to the office."

"Isn't the listening device evidence enough?" she asked.

"It proves someone was listening in to what happened at the main house but the rest is circumstantial," he said, making quick work of the food on his plate.

Despite thinking there was no way she could eat, she cleaned her plate in a matter of minutes too. It was always easy to tell when good food was served because conversation slowed to a stop.

"It's easy to connect the dots," she said.

"I'd say it casts suspicion more than anything else," he admitted. "Even if by some miracle Lawler is able to lift a print off the device found in the main house and connect it back to one of my family members, it still doesn't link them to the actual crimes. We would need a fingerprint here at Meg's house or on your car for that."

"What do you think?" she asked.

"I haven't been home in so long I don't know what to think," he said. "The other side of the family has become essentially strangers to me in the years that I've been gone. I'm almost embarrassed to admit that I barely know my brothers anymore. I'm just going on what I used to know of them. The few I've spoken to since I got back seem like grown versions of the people I knew."

"Can I ask a question?" She'd been wanting to ever since the other night.

"Go ahead," he said before finishing off his cup of coffee. "You get one shot."

"Why didn't you come home? I mean, there were holidays and I'm sure you had leave," she said, checking to make sure she wasn't wandering into dangerous territory. He didn't seem too upset by the line of questioning. "Didn't you miss being with your family?"

"I needed to grow up," he said. "I couldn't do that if I was constantly coming home where everything was familiar."

"And you couldn't grow up in Lone Star Pass with your family?" she asked.

"I didn't think so at the time," he admitted.

"Have you changed your mind now?" she continued.

"It was the right choice for me at the time. I have no question about it," he said. "It's hard to explain but my family overtakes a person. My family name meant nothing to anyone overseas. I was just one of the guys out there. Here, you can already see the kind of drama going on that sucks a person in and dominates their life. Of course, before the Marshall died it wasn't quite this bad. Now, it's everyone's worst fear realized."

"And you wish you were still overseas?"

17

Fallon couldn't say what was really on his mind, that he wanted to be right where he was. The admission caught him off guard. It had nothing to do with the drama at the ranch and everything to do with the woman sitting at the table.

His cell buzzed, which got him out of answering the question directly. He had a policy about being honest. He'd rather avoid answering altogether than stretch the truth.

"It's Eric," he said, fishing out his cell and then checking the screen. "I should take this call."

She nodded before standing up and collecting the breakfast dishes.

"Hey, what did you find out?" he asked.

"It's there. I found the desk calendar," Eric said. "You're never going to believe this. The person he'd been spending the most time with was Aunt Jackie."

"Well, that's an interesting fact," Fallon said. A picture was emerging. One that didn't look good.

"She's made no secret of her spending habits," Eric said.

"Mom said the woman spends more money than some small countries."

"On what?" Fallon asked, curiosity getting the best of him. What she bought was probably not relevant.

"Mom says she has expensive taste," Eric said. "I'm guessing clothes, shoes, travel. I have no idea and never really thought to ask."

"Could she be in on something with Uncle Keif?" Fallon asked.

"Your guess is as good as mine," Eric said.

"What about our cousins? Could one or a few of them be in on it?" Fallon asked.

"I can't imagine it," Eric stated. "It's possible she could have tainted one of them against us. More than that? I just can't imagine it happening without word getting out. Someone would talk and you know how that would end up."

"Has Lawler interviewed all of our cousins?" Fallon asked.

"I imagine so by now," Eric supplied. "If he didn't before, he certainly will be doing so today. I'm texting him as we speak. Figured I'd give you a heads up first."

"Lawler will want to speak to Harlen to confirm his suspicions," Fallon continued.

The call went dead quiet.

"Fallon..." Eric's voice took a dive.

"What is it?" Fallon asked.

"Lawler just responded that several of our cousins have gone missing, as well as Aunt Jackie," he said.

"What about Uncle Keif?" Fallon asked.

"He said they decided to head out of town for a few days until this whole ordeal blew over. Everyone took separate vehicles, though. Uncle Keif stuck around for questioning,"

Eric continued. "Lawler thinks Uncle Keif is hiding something."

"What's the next step?" Fallon asked.

"Lawler has asked everyone to come home and to come into his office for questioning tomorrow morning," Eric stated.

"And?"

"Uncle Keif said that's impossible because they didn't take their cell phones," Eric said.

"Not exactly the actions of innocent people," Fallon stated.

"My thoughts exactly," Eric confirmed. "Uncle Keif said the stress of the investigation is getting to his family and the harassment has to stop. He claimed they had rights and if the sheriff wasn't there to arrest anyone, he needed to get out and get off the property."

"I'm sure that didn't go over very well." Fallon wished he'd been a fly on that wall.

"Lawler reminded him that he was standing on our side of the family's property and Uncle Keif had no right to kick him out," Eric said, then paused for a long moment. "Hey, be careful while we have so many questions and no answers."

"I've defended myself against an unknown enemy before," Fallon reassured.

"This one might know us better than we think," Eric stated.

They ended the call with both of them agreeing to watch their backs, and everyone else's too.

BEFORE BIRDIE KNEW IT, the sun had gone down. The day had been a blaze of caretakers coming for Meg, others to help with the house, and the sit down meals that she, Meg, and Fallon had had together.

"This has been one of the best days I've had in a long time." Meg smiled up at Birdie as she sat on the edge of her bed.

"That's good to hear," Birdie said. It had been a long time since she'd seen Meg this happy. After Christopher left, it had felt like a downward slide until she'd become so sick it was almost as though she'd given up. "We're going to have many more days like this one."

"I know you wish I'd stick around forever, sweet girl," Meg started. "But I'm ready."

"What if I'm not?" Birdie said, wishing she hadn't been so blunt but needing to be honest.

"You have your whole life in front of you." Meg patted Birdie's hand. "Sticking around here taking care of an old woman isn't what you should be doing at your age."

"What if I love being with you?" Birdie asked, trying to blink the tears away.

"There's no question that I love every minute of time we have together." Meg sighed. "I just don't want to be a ball and chain."

"You couldn't be," Birdie said. Was that the reason Meg said those things? She didn't want to be a burden? "Hang in there, okay?"

"Wouldn't dream of leaving you alone with that handsome man in the next room," Meg quipped. "I'm pregnant just looking at him."

Birdie laughed out loud.

"I get to be your only baby, Meg," Birdie responded with a smile.

"You better not leave me alone with your boyfriend, or I'll have no problem stealing him away from you," Meg said.

At least the spark was back in her eyes, a spark Birdie hadn't seen in far too long.

"I'll keep that in mind," she said, figuring that was easier than explaining she wasn't in a relationship with Fallon.

Birdie pushed up to standing, turning the light off on her way out of the room.

"This was a good day for Meg," she said to Fallon. The man standing in Meg's kitchen was gorgeous. He would probably laugh at being called that, but it was true.

His cell buzzed and he checked the screen.

"Security is coming to give an update," he said. "Do you want to come outside with me?"

"I'll be out in a minute," she stated. "I'll just finish cleaning up in here."

The sound of the door opening in the next room was followed by a grunt. A lamp crashed to the floor. Birdie bolted toward the sound.

FALLON HAD BEEN CAUGHT off guard. He had no weapon within reach, except for the lamp. On his side, curled in a ball to protect his internal organs, he reached for the base of the lamp.

"No, sir." The five-feet-two-inch security personnel stomped on his wrist. He heard a crack sound and prayed it wasn't a bone. All he saw was a blurry vision of her ponytail as it swished. She'd knocked him upside the head with a baton. And as he stepped toward her, a second person entered the picture. Two on one when he was caught off guard wasn't the kind of odds he preferred.

Ignoring the pain shooting up his arm, he withdrew his hand. Without warning, he rolled onto his back and did a kip-up, hopping to his feet. In the next second, he fired off a roundhouse, nailing Guard Two on the chin. Spit squirted from his mouth as his head snapped to one side.

"Call 911," he shouted to Birdie. "Lock yourself in Meg's room and make the call."

Knowing she'd been in the kitchen a few moments before, he hoped she could hear him.

And then Ponytail disappeared around the corner at the same time Guard Two sucker-punched Fallon in the gut. He bent forward, and then popped back up. He stepped into Guard Two, who was a few inches shorter and slighter framed, and head-butted the man.

Despite the fact Fallon was going to have a serious headache later, the move was worth it. Concern for Birdie was a gut punch. But he had to subdue Guard Two before he could do anything else.

Grabbing the lamp, he wrapped the chord around Guard Two's neck until he passed out. He grabbed the hand-cuffs from the man's belt, and then cuffed his hands behind his back after taking his jacket with the security company logo on it. Fallon checked for a pulse, got one.

He surveyed the house for any signs or sounds of Birdie as he put on the jacket, but it was quiet.

Fallon bolted toward the kitchen. No one was there. She couldn't have passed by him. And then he heard it. A grunt from the backyard. He bolted out there in time to see Pony-tail dragging a fighting Birdie across the lawn. Toward the van?

In a swift motion, he came up behind Ponytail. This time, he had the element of surprise on his side. He wrapped one arm around her neck and covered her mouth with his free hand. The chokehold did the trick, and her body fell limp to the ground.

"Put this on," he said to Birdie, tossing the security jacket to her. "I don't know who else is in the van, but they've been watching us."

He grabbed Ponytail's handcuffs and cuffed her hands behind her back, leaving her slumped on her side.

Birdie took the belt from Ponytail, and they rounded the corner of the house to where the van was parked. A black luxury sedan was parked behind the van but there was no one inside. Fallon approached the van with caution. He opened the door to a very surprised-looking face.

"Aunt Jackie?" he said. He turned to Birdie. "Did you make the call?"

Aunt Jackie tried to bolt out the back door. He dove inside the van and knocked her onto the hard floor.

"You're not going anywhere," he said. "Except jail."

Fallon wrangled her hands behind her back. "We can sit here all night, or you can tell me why you did it."

She shook her head.

"Money?" he asked, figuring she'd promised his security detail a cut of the profits to get them to turn. He never did completely trust civilians. Now, he realized his instincts had been right all along.

"Your grandfather was going to cut us out of the will altogether," Aunt Jackie bit out. "After everything we've done for him. It wasn't fair. He was a selfish old geezer."

"How could you do this to your own family?" he asked, not bothering to hide his disgust. Firebrands were loyal people, at least they used to be. He also wondered if there would ever be a way to put the pieces of this fractured family back together.

"You would do the same thing if you were in my position," she scoffed.

"No, Aunt Jackie, I wouldn't. Honor is the difference

between you and me. And I never would try to take something that didn't belong to me," he said.

"Your grandfather didn't need all that money, and your father is worthless," she spit out. "He's just as bad as the old man was."

Fallon couldn't say whether she was right or wrong on that count. But finding out could wait. Because Aunt Jackie was going to prison, and he had something he needed to say to Birdie.

~

BIRDIE SAT ON THE PORCH, watching as the last of the law enforcement vehicles pulled away. Fallon was walking toward her after giving his final statement. Curious neighbors had already retreated back inside their home. Thankfully, Meg slept through the entire ordeal. She would wake up tomorrow without a care in the world.

"Hey," Fallon said, stopping in front of her. He reached out and took her hands in his and then pulled her up to standing.

"Hey there," she said to him right back. This was probably the part where he told her that it had been real but it was time for him to bolt.

"Are you okay?" he asked, glancing at what was probably going to be a shiner on her left eye. Hey, she'd gotten off a good shot in the face on Ponytail, as Fallon called her. The woman's training had kicked in, and she'd kicked Birdie's butt. She'd been no match, but it sure felt good to know she'd still cold-cocked a trained guard.

"Surprisingly good," she said to him, to this beautiful man. His leaving was going to do a number on her heart.

She took in a breath and readied herself for the goodbye that was surely coming. "Except…"

She let her voice trail off when he locked gazes with her and held. There was something stirring in his eyes that she couldn't quite pinpoint. An emotion that had him looking torn.

"I want to sleep with you tonight," he said. "And I want to wake up with you in my arms tomorrow."

Birdie's mouth nearly hit the lawn.

"You don't 'do' sleepovers, Fallon," she said, not really sure why she'd just reminded him of the fact.

"Nope. I don't," he said, locking onto her gaze.

And then it dawned on her what she saw in his eyes…it was something that looked a whole lot like love. But could it be?

"Then, what changed your mind?" she asked.

"You," he said without skipping a beat. "I've dated around for a long time. I know what I want and what I don't. I want to sleep with you and wake up with you. I want to be with you every day because, as shocking as this might sound, I've fallen in love with you. But we can start slow. We can do this however you want. All I know for certain is that I want to be in your life in any capacity you'll let me. I love you, Birdie."

Those were the rawest, sweetest words she'd ever heard.

"I hope you don't snore too loudly," she said with a smile. "But if you do, I'll just have to get used to it."

"Does that mean what I think?" he asked.

She nodded before pushing up to her tiptoes and kissing her man. When she pulled back this time, she said, "I'm in love with you, Fallon. I want to do forever with you."

"Good, because 'for the rest of your life' is what I'm asking," he said.

"I'll take that deal," she said, her heart singing in her chest. "And seal it with a kiss."

Birdie looped her arms around the neck of the man she planned to spend forever with and kissed him until she couldn't tell where she ended and he began as their hearts melded together forever.

"Welcome home," Grayson Firebrand said to his brother Fallon, who brought him into a bear hug. Fallon had been home less than a month and this was the first time Grayson laid eyes on his brother and his new wife.

"It's good to be back," Fallon said. "And good to see you again as much as I hate to admit it."

Grayson laughed. The ranch had seen so many ups and downs this summer he was beginning to believe he'd been strapped onto a never-ending roller coaster. Despite the intense heat, fall was around the corner.

"Nice to officially meet you," he said, turning to his newly minted sister-in-law.

"You too," Birdie said before adding, "Your brother has told me a lot about you. It's nice to finally meet."

"Welcome to the family," Grayson said, ushering the new couple into the kitchen of the main house. "How about a round of coffee?"

"Was that a serious question?" Birdie teased. He liked her already.

This was the first time he'd seen his brother in more than a decade, but he'd never known Fallon to be this happy. The night before he'd left for bootcamp, Grayson had asked him why.

His brother had responded with a simple answer, "I don't know who I am without all of this."

Grayson fixed and poured three cups before setting them on the island. The way his brother looked at his new bride reminded Grayson of everything that had been missing in his own relationships over the past few years. It didn't bother him, though. Being in a relationship was about the last thing on his mind after losing Savannah. A voice in the back of his head picked that moment to remind him that she'd been gone two years. It was two years, three months, and twenty-six days to be exact.

"How is your grandmother?" Grayson asked Birdie.

"Surprisingly stable," she said with a smile. "She's working on her art again and that has always made her the happiest."

"Moving here on the ranch with Birdie and me seems to be giving her a renewed lease on life," Fallon said.

"That's great news." Grayson understood Meg's condition was diagnosed as terminal, but miracles happened. Not in his life, he figured. Or Savannah would still be alive. "You never really know how much time you have with someone. It's important to make the best of every day."

Grayson heard the melancholy in his own voice. He tried to cover with a cough, but not much got past Fallon. Based on the way his brother studied Grayson, Fallon was onto something.

"Good news about Dad's recovery," Fallon said after taking a sip of coffee. He'd always had a sixth sense when Grayson slipped into a dark place despite never knowing the situation he'd been in. Grayson had never been much of a talker. And he'd never told anyone in the family that he'd been in a relationship. By the time he realized he loved her, she was gone.

"It sure is," Grayson did his level best to shake off the dark cloud threatening to consume him. He'd worked long hours on the ranch and volunteered for every extra assignment he could to keep himself busy. He couldn't wonder if this pain would ever end.

"Have you heard from the other side of the family yet?" Fallon asked.

"Uncle Keif is beside himself from all accounts. A few of our cousins have reached out to make certain we know they had nothing to do with the plot to alter the will. Based on the investigation, it's looking very much like Aunt Jackie acted alone." Grayson shook his head.

"It has to be the worst for them," Fallon said. "I never liked her much, but that's their mother."

"The timing isn't right, but we have to figure out a way to get this whole family in the same room to talk," Grayson said.

"Wishful thinking, bro," Fallon stated.

"You're probably right," Grayson said. "Uncle Keif stopped over to visit Dad, though."

Fallon's jaw nearly dropped to the floor. "That's a miracle."

"He stayed for a few minutes at least," Grayson added. Hope was probably too much to ask for. Instead, he settled on being happy his brother had come home. At least his side of the family was finally together again. One by one, his brothers were getting married. They seemed happy.

Good for them, he thought. That road wasn't meant for everyone.

. . .

FIND out if Grayson ever takes a bride here.

ALSO BY BARB HAN

Texas Firebrand

Rancher to the Rescue

Disarming the Rancher

Rancher under Fire

Rancher on the Line

Undercover with the Rancher

Rancher in Danger

Set-up with the Rancher

Don't Mess With Texas Cowboys

Texas Cowboy's Protection

Texas Cowboy Justice

Texas Cowboy's Honor

Texas Cowboy Daddy

Texas Cowboy's Baby

Texas Cowboy's Bride

Texas Cowboy's Family

Cowboys of Cattle Cove

Cowboy Reckoning

Cowboy Cover-up

Cowboy Retribution

Cowboy Judgment

Cowboy Conspiracy

For more of Barb's books, visit www.BarbHan.com.

ABOUT THE AUTHOR

Barb Han is a USA TODAY and Publisher's Weekly Best-selling Author. Reviewers have called her books "heartfelt" and "exciting."

Barb lives in Texas—her true north—with her adventurous family, a poodle mix and a spunky rescue who is often referred to as a hot mess. She is the proud owner of too many books (if there is such a thing). When not writing, she can be found exploring Manhattan, on a mountain either hiking or skiing depending on the season, or swimming in her own backyard.

Sign up for Barb's newsletter at www.BarbHan.com.

Printed in Great Britain
by Amazon

69875071R00111